The desperation in Faith's voice turned Travis inside out.

He longed to hold her close and whisper that everything would be all right, but it would be an empty promise. And once she was in his arms with her soft body pressed into his, comfort wouldn't be the only thing on his mind.

He wanted to kiss her, had wanted to since the night he'd first laid eyes on her in the Passion Pit, though he hadn't admitted that to himself then.

Now the desire was entangled with his need to keep her safe and help her find her son.

HARD RIDE TO DRY GULCH

—

Joanna Wayne

H HARLEQUIN® INTRIGUE®

Recycling programs for this product may not exist in your area.

A special salute to mothers everywhere who know what it's like to love a child unconditionally. A smile to my grandchildren who bring endless joy to my life. And hats off to my editor, Denise Zaza, who has worked with me through almost sixty books. Here's to sixty more.

ISBN-13: 978-0-373-69771-7

HARD RIDE TO DRY GULCH

Copyright © 2014 by Jo Ann Vest

Printed in U.S.A.

www.Harlequin.com

ABOUT THE AUTHOR

Joanna Wayne was born and raised in Shreveport, Louisiana, and received her undergraduate and graduate degrees from LSU Shreveport. She moved to New Orleans in 1984, and it was there that she attended her first writing class and joined her first professional writing organization. Her debut novel, *Deep in the Bayou*, was published in 1994.

Now, dozens of published books later, Joanna has made a name for herself as being on the cutting edge of romantic suspense in both series and single-title novels. She has been on the Waldenbooks bestseller list for romance and has won many industry awards. She is also a popular speaker at writing organizations and local community functions and has taught creative writing at the University of New Orleans Metropolitan College.

Joanna currently resides in a small community forty miles north of Houston, Texas, with her husband. Though she still has many family and emotional ties to Louisiana, she loves living in the Lone Star State. You may write Joanna at P.O. Box 852, Montgomery, Texas 77356.

Books by Joanna Wayne

HARLEQUIN INTRIGUE

CAST OF CHARACTERS

Faith Ashburn—When her 18-year-old son goes missing, she will stop at nothing to find him.

Travis Dalton—Houston homicide detective. Once he meets Faith, he will do anything to help her find her son and keep Faith safe.

Reuben Jackson Dalton, better known as R.J.—Travis's father and the owner of the Dry Gulch Ranch.

Cornell Ashburn—Faith's missing son.

Reno Vargas—Travis's partner.

Georgio Trosclair—Owner of the Passion Pit.

Angela Pointer—Exotic dancer who was involved with Cornell.

Mark Ethridge—Head of the DPD missing persons division.

John Patterson—Border patrol agent and a friend of Travis.

Walt Marshall—Former boyfriend of Angela Pointer.

Alex Salinger—Rancher in Laredo.

Joni Dalton—Best friend of Faith Ashburn, and Travis's new sister-in-law.

Leif Dalton—Joni's husband.

Alex and Hadley Dalton—Son and daughter-in-law of R.J., who live on the Dry Gulch Ranch.

Lila and Lacy Dalton—Twin daughters of Alex and Hadley.

Effie Dalton—Leif Dalton's teenage daughter.

Prologue

Faith Ashburn emphasized her deep-set brown eyes with a coat of thick black liner and then took a step away from the mirror to see the full effect of the makeup she'd caked onto her pale skin. The haunted eyes that stared back at her were the only part of the face she recognized.

Her irises mirrored the way she felt. Lost. Trapped in a nightmare. The anxiety so intense the lining of her stomach seemed to be on fire.

But she'd go back out there tonight, into the smoke and groping, the stares that crawled across her skin like hairy spiders. She'd smile and endure the depravity—praying, always praying for some crumb of information that would lead her to her son.

Cornell was eighteen now. Physically, he was a man. Mentally and emotionally, he was a kid, at least he was in her mind. A trusting, naive boy who needed his mother and his meds.

Faith's bare feet sank into the thick mauve carpet as she stepped back into her bedroom and tugged on her patterned panty hose. Then she pulled the low-cut, trampy black dress from the closet and stepped into it.

The fabric stretched over her bare breasts as she slid the spaghetti straps over her narrow shoulders. Her nipples were covered, but there was enough cleavage showing to suggest that she'd have no qualms about revealing everything if the offer appealed to her.

Reaching to the top shelf of her closet, she chose the bright red stiletto heels. They never failed to garner the instant attention of men high on booze, drugs and the stench of overripe sex.

Struck by a burst of vertigo, Faith held on to the bedpost until the dizziness passed. Then she tucked a lipstick, her car keys and some mad money into the small sequined handbag that already held her licensed pistol.

Stopping off in the kitchen, she poured two fingers of cheap whiskey into a glass. She swished the amber liquid around in her mouth, gargled and then spit it down the drain. Holding the glass over the sink, she ran one finger around the edges to collect the remaining liquor. She dotted it at her pulse points like expensive perfume.

Her muscles clenched. Her lungs clogged. She took a deep breath and walked out the door, carefully locking it behind her.

Six months of going unofficially undercover into the seediest areas of Dallas. Six months of questioning every drug addict and pervert that might have come in contact with Cornell, based on nothing but the one shrapnel of evidence the police had provided her.

Six months of crying herself to sleep when she came home as lost, confused and desperate as before.

God, please let tonight be different.

"ANOTHER BACKSTREET HOMICIDE, another trip to see Georgio. I'm beginning to think he gives a discount to killers. A lap dance from one of his girls when a body shows up at the morgue without identification."

"And the victims get younger and younger." Travis Dalton followed his partner, Reno, as they walked through a side door of the sleaziest strip joint in the most dangerous part of Dallas. Georgio reigned as king here, providing the local sex and drug addicts with everything they needed to feed their cravings.

Yet the rotten bastard always came out on top. His rule of threats and intimidation eliminated any chance of getting one of his patrons to testify against him. Not that they would have had a shred of credibility if they had.

A rap song blared from the sound system as a couple of seminude women with surgery-enhanced butts and breasts made love to skinny poles. Two others gyrated around the rim of the stage, collecting bills in their G-strings.

A familiar waitress whose name Travis couldn't remember sashayed up to him. "Business or pleasure, copper boy?"

"What do you think?"

"Business, but a girl can hope. Are you looking for Georgio?"

"For starters."

"Is it about that boy who got shot up in Oak Cliff last night?"

Now she had Travis's full attention. "What do you know about that?"

"Nothing, I just figured that's what brought you here."

Travis had a hunch she knew more than she was admitting. He was about to question her further when he noticed a woman at the bar trying to peel a man's grip from her right wrist.

"Let go of me," she said, her voice rising above the din.

The man held tight while his free hand groped her breast. "I just want to be friends."

"You're hurting me."

Travis stormed to the bar. "You heard the woman. Move on, buddy."

"Why don't you mind your own business?"

"I am." He pulled the ID from the breast pocket of his blue pullover. "Dallas Police. Back off or I snap a nice metal bracelet on your wrist and haul you down to central lockup."

A thin stream of spittle made its way down the man's whiskered chin as his hands fell to his sides. Wiping it away with his shirtsleeve, he slid off the barstool and stumbled backward.

"She's the one you should be arresting. She came on to me," he slurred.

Travis studied the woman and decided the drunk could be right. She was flaunting the trappings of a hooker, right down to a sexy pair of heels that made her shapely legs appear a mile long.

But one look into her haunted eyes and Travis doubted she was looking to make a fast buck on her back. She had a delicate, fragile quality about her that suggested she'd be more at home in a convent than here shoving off drunks. Even the exaggerated makeup couldn't hide her innocence.

If he had to guess, he'd say she was here trying to get even with some jerk who had cheated on her. That didn't make it any less dangerous for her to be in this hellhole.

"Party's over, lady. I'm calling for a squad car to take you home."

"I have a car."

"Get behind the wheel and I'll have to arrest you for driving while intoxicated."

"I'm not drunk."

He couldn't argue that point. She smelled like a distillery, but she wasn't slurring her words and her eyes were clear, her pupils normal.

"I don't know what kind of game you're playing or

who you're trying to get even with, but if you hang around here, you're going to run into more trouble than you can handle."

"I can take care of myself." She turned and started to walk away.

Travis moved quicker, setting himself in her path without realizing why he was bothering.

He looked around for Reno, but his partner wasn't in sight. He was probably already questioning Georgio, and Travis should be with him.

"Look, lady. You're in over your head here. I've got some urgent business, but sit tight for a few minutes and I'll be back to walk you to your car. In the meantime, don't make friends with any more perverts. That's an order."

She shrugged and nodded.

He stalked off to find Reno. He spotted him and Georgio a minute later near the door to the suite of private offices. When he looked back, the woman was gone.

Just as well, he told himself, especially if she'd gone home. He didn't need any more problems tonight. But even after he reached Reno and jumped into the murderous situation at hand, he couldn't fully shake her from his mind.

Whatever had brought her slumming could get her killed.

Chapter One

Four months later

Travis adjusted the leather-and-turquoise bolo tie, a close match to the one his brother was wearing with his Western-style tux. The irony of seeing his formerly Armani-faithful attorney brother dressed like this made it hard for Travis not to laugh.

"I never thought I'd see the day you got hitched to a cowgirl."

"I never thought I'd see the day you showed up at the Dry Gulch Ranch again," Leif answered.

"Couldn't miss the wedding of my favorite brother."

"Your *only* brother."

"Yeah, probably a good thing you don't have competition now that you're building a house here on the ranch. On the bright side, I do like that I get to wear my cowboy boots with this rented monkey suit."

Travis rocked back on the heels of his new boots, bought for the conspicuous occasion of Leif's wedding to Joni Griffin. He'd never seen his brother happier. Not only was he so in love that he beamed when he looked at his veterinarian bride, but his daughter, Effie, would be living with him for her last two years of high school.

The Dry Gulch Ranch was spiffed up for the ceremony

and reception. Lights were strung through the branches of giant oaks and stringy sycamores. A white tent had been set up with chairs, leaving a makeshift aisle that led to a rose-covered altar where the two lovers would take their vows.

Most of the chairs were taken. Leif's friends from the prestigious law firm from which he'd recently resigned to open his own office nearer the ranch mingled with what looked to be half the population of Oak Grove.

The women from both groups looked quite elegant. The Big D lawyers were all in designer suits. The ranchers for the most part looked as if they'd feel a lot more at home in their Wranglers than in their off-the-rack suits and choking ties.

In fact, a few of the younger cowboys were in jeans and sport coats. Travis figured they were the smart ones. Weekends he wasn't working a homicide case he usually spent on a friend's ranch up in the hill country.

Riding, roping, baling hay, branding—he'd done it all and loved it. A weekend place on the Dry Gulch Ranch, just a little over an hour from Dallas, would have been the perfect solution to Travis. Except for one very large problem.

Rueben Jackson Dalton, his father by virtue of a healthy sperm.

"Time for us to join the preacher," Leif said, jerking Travis back into the moment.

He walked at his brother's side and felt a momentary sense of anxiety. He and Leif had been through hell together growing up, most caused by R.J.

It had been just the two of them against the world since their mother's death, and they'd always been as close as a horse to a saddle. Now Leif was marrying and moving onto R.J.'s spread.

Oh, hell, what was he worried about? R.J. would never come between him and Leif. Besides, the old coot would be dead soon.

The music started. Leif's fifteen-year-old daughter started down the aisle, looking so grown-up Travis felt his chest constrict. He could only imagine what the sight did to Leif. Travis winked at Effie as she took her place at the altar. Her smile was so big it took over her face and danced in her eyes.

Travis looked up again and did a double take as he spotted the maid of honor gliding down the aisle. She damn sure didn't look the way she did the last time he'd seen her, but there was no doubt in his mind that the gorgeous lady was the same one he'd rescued in Georgio's sleaziest strip club four months earlier.

He'd spent only a few minutes with her, but she'd preyed on his mind a lot since then, so much so that he found himself showing up at Georgio's palace of perversion even when his work didn't call for doing so.

All in the interest of talking to her and making sure she was safe. In spite of his efforts, he'd never caught sight of her again.

Travis studied the woman as she took her place a few feet away from him. She was absolutely stunning in a luscious creation the color of the amethyst ring his mother used to wear. She'd given the ring to him before she'd died.

It was the only prized possession Travis owned—well, that and the belt buckles he'd won in bull-riding competitions back when he had more guts than sense.

The wedding march sounded. The guests all stood. Travis's eyes remained fixed on the maid of honor. Finally, she looked at him, and when their eyes met, he saw the same tortured, haunting depths that had mesmerized him at their first meeting.

Travis forced his gaze away from the mystery woman and back to Joni and Travis. He wouldn't spoil the wedding, but before the night was over he'd have a little chat with the seductive maid of honor. Before he was through, he'd discover if she was as innocent as he'd first believed, or if the demons who'd filled her eyes with anguish had actually driven her to the dark side of life.

If the latter was the case, he'd make damn sure she stayed away from his niece, even if it meant telling Leif the truth about his new wife's best friend.

The reception might have a lot more spectacular fireworks than originally planned. Travis was already itching for the first dance.

Chapter Two

So far, so good, Faith decided as she concentrated on putting one foot in front of the other. She had to hold it together and not let her emotions careen out of control. Any tears shed tonight should be ones of joy.

Unfortunately, she'd forgotten what joy felt like. Cornell had been missing for ten months now and she seemed no closer to finding him. Her nerves were ragged, her emotions so unsteady that the slightest incident could set off the waterworks.

Had it been anyone else who'd asked her to be maid of honor in her wedding, Faith could easily have said no. But she couldn't refuse Joni, especially after the way Joni had stood by her when Cornell first went missing.

Joni was still concerned, but as the weeks had turned into months, she—like Faith's other friends—had moved on with their lives. Faith understood, though she could never move on until Cornell was home again and safe.

As for the cops' theory that Cornell had left home by choice, she was convinced it was pure bunk. Sure, she could buy that Cornell had gotten mixed up with the wrong crowd. He was extremely vulnerable to peer influence.

And she wasn't so naive as to believe it was impossible

that he might have experimented with drugs. A lot of kids had by age eighteen. But never in a million years would Cornell have left home and shut her out of his life—not of his own free will.

Wherever he was tonight, he was being held against his will or—

Here she went again, working herself into an anxiety-fueled meltdown.

This was Joni's big night. Surely Faith could hold herself together for a couple hours.

Her glance settled on Leif Dalton. A boyish grin split his lips, and his dark eyes danced in anticipation. A sexy, loving cowboy waiting for his beautiful bride. Joni was a very lucky woman—if it lasted.

For Faith, marriage had been one of life's major disappointments, enough so that she had no intention of ever tying the knot again.

She switched her concentration to Leif's brother and best man. Tall. Thick, dark hair that fell playfully over his forehead. Hard bodied. Ruggedly handsome.

And familiar.

She struggled to figure out where she'd seen him before as she took her place on the other side of Leif's daughter. Faith had missed the rehearsal celebration last night and arrived at the ranch only minutes before the ceremony tonight.

But she'd definitely seen him somewhere.

The tempo of the music changed and a second later the bridal march filled the air. Sounds of shuffling feet and whispered oohs and aahs filled the air as the guests rose to their feet for their first sight of Joni in her white satin-and-lace gown.

Adorable twin girls, their curly red hair topped with pink bows, skipped and danced down the aisle in front of

Joni, scattering rose petals. Lila and Lacy, Leif's three-year-old half nieces, whom Joni bragged about continuously. Faith wouldn't be surprised if Leif and Joni didn't start a family of their own within the year.

Faith stole another quick glance at the best man. Her heart pounded.

All of a sudden she knew exactly where she'd seen him before. In a Dallas strip club. He was the sexy cop who'd come to her rescue a few months back. The cop whose orders she'd disobeyed when she'd cleared out before he could ask too many questions.

He wouldn't be nearly as easy to dodge tonight.

Talk about spoiling a wedding. One word from the groom's brother about where he'd met the slutty maid of honor and Joni would figure out exactly why Faith had turned down every Saturday-night invitation to meet her and Leif for dinner.

Joni would worry about Faith's safety. Worse, if she couldn't persuade Faith to give up her visits to the criminal underbelly of Dallas, she'd insist on getting involved. No way could Faith drag Joni into that.

Steady, girl. Don't panic.

There was a good chance the hunky, nosy cop wouldn't connect her to the woman he'd met in a strip club months ago. For one thing, she had on tons less makeup. For another, she wasn't braless. She was just Joni's maid of honor.

Besides, he'd originally figured her for just another woman on the make, or perhaps even one of the off-duty strippers. No reason for him to have given her another thought.

Play this cool, leave at the first opportunity, and the cop would never guess they'd ever met.

"SURELY YOU'RE NOT thinking of sneaking out without a dance with the best man?"

The husky male voice startled Faith. Poor timing. She'd already stepped out of the tent and was about to start down the path to the parked cars.

Except for a brief conversation when Leif had introduced them after the ceremony, she'd managed to avoid Travis all evening.

She flashed what she hoped was an innocent-looking smile. "I'm not sneaking anywhere. I've said my good-byes to the happy couple."

"It's still early. The party is in full swing."

"Yes, but it's a long drive back to Dallas."

"So why drive it? The guest rooms in the newlyweds' ranch bungalow aren't fully finished yet, but I'm sure R.J. can put you up for the night. From what I've seen of his house, there are plenty of spare bedrooms."

"So I've heard. Joni invited me to stay over," Faith admitted. "But I really need to get home tonight."

The band returned from their break. A guitar strummed. The lead female singer in the country-and-western band that had kept the portable dance floor occupied all night belted out the first words to an old Patsy Cline hit.

Travis fitted a hand to the small of Faith's back. "One dance before you call it a night?"

Her brain issued a warning, but the music, the night and even the tiny lights that twinkled above them like stars overpowered her caution. Besides, Travis showed no sign of recognizing her. What could one dance hurt?

They walked back to the dance floor together. His arms slid around her, pulling her close as their bodies began to sway to the haunting ballad. His cheek brushed hers. An unfamiliar heat shimmered deep inside her. She dissolved into the sensual sensations for mere seconds before her brain kicked in again.

She hadn't felt a man's arms around her for years. No wonder her body had reacted to the contact.

She pulled away, putting an inch of space between her breasts and his chest and points lower. The warmth didn't fully dissipate, but her breathing came easier.

By the time they finished the dance, she was almost fully in control. "I really do have to go now," she said, leading the way as they left the dance floor.

"If you must."

"I must. And really, there's no reason for you to walk me to my car."

"A promise is a promise."

The man was persistent. If the cops handling Cornell's missing-person case had been half as determined, they likely would have located him by now.

"No reason for you to leave the reception," she said. "I'm sure I can find my way to my car on my own."

"But what kind of gentleman would I be if I let you?"

"A sensible one."

"Not my strong suit."

"I got here late and had to park in the pasture across the road. You'll get those gorgeous boots of yours dirty," she said.

"I'll risk it."

Further protests would sound ungrateful or just plain pigheaded. Besides, it would be a lot darker once they left the twinkling lights. Her car could be difficult to locate among all the other vehicles. Travis might just come in handy.

Reaching into the petite jeweled evening bag that swung from her shoulder, she took out the keys to her aging Honda and started walking. Their shoulders brushed. A zing of awareness shot through her.

Disgusted with herself for letting Travis affect her, she picked up her pace. Bad call. Maneuvering the grass and uneven ground in her six-inch stilettos proved to be a dangerous balancing act.

The second time she almost tripped, she was forced to accept the arm Travis offered for support. A traitorous flutter appeared in her stomach.

It had to be just her nerves, or the fact that Travis was several cuts above the perverts she'd been spending her time with. Not every night the way she had in the beginning, but every weekend.

A breeze stirred. Faith looked up and was struck by the brilliance of the stars now that they'd left the artificial illumination.

"Amazing, aren't they?" Travis said, apparently noticing her fascination with the heavens.

"Yes. Hard to believe those are the same stars that appear over Dallas. They look so much closer here."

"Nothing like getting out in the wide-open spaces to appreciate the splendor of nature," Travis agreed.

"Do you spend much time out here?"

"At the Dry Gulch? No way."

"I guess that will change now that Leif will be living out here."

"It won't change anytime soon."

"Because of your relationship with your father?"

"You got it. And you apparently know a lot more about me, Faith Ashburn, than I do about you."

"Joni told me a bit about why you and Leif have issues with R.J. But Leif changed his mind about his father. Perhaps you will, too."

"Sure, and Texas might vote to outlaw beef."

"Stranger things have happened."

"Not in my lifetime," Travis countered. "But it was a beautiful wedding."

"I've never seen Joni so radiant."

"Have you and Joni been friends long?"

"Eight years. We met in a psychology class at Oklahoma University. We clicked immediately and became fast friends even though I was divorced and had a young son."

They made small talk until she spotted her car and unlocked it with her remote device. The lights blinked. "That's my Honda," she said, grateful for an excuse to end the conversation before he started asking personal questions again.

She let go of Travis's arm and hurried toward her car.

Travis kept pace, then stepped in front of her at the last minute, blocking the driver's side door. "You know, Faith, you look a lot better without all that makeup you were wearing the first time we met."

Her mouth grew dry, her chest tight. "I don't know what you're talking about. I've never seen you before tonight."

"Actually, we met a few months ago. You're not the kind of woman a man could forget."

Faith wondered at what point during the night he'd figured that out. She shrugged. "Sorry. You must have me confused with someone else."

"Not a chance." He propped his left hand against the car roof and leaned in closer. "Let me refresh your memory. The Passion Pit. Four months ago. You were cruising the bar when one of your admirers got out of hand."

She rolled her eyes. "Cruising the bar?"

"Don't go all naive on me, Faith. A lady doesn't just drop into the Passion Pit unescorted because she's thirsty.

You were wearing a black dress that left little to the imagination and a pair of nosebleed heels that screamed to be noticed. We talked. I asked you to wait so that I could see you safely home. You didn't."

"You definitely have me confused with someone else."

"Not unless you have an identical twin. I asked Joni. She assured me you don't."

And Faith was a terrible liar. That left truth or some version of it as her only feasible choice if she wanted to get the detective off her back.

"You're right." She cast her eyes downward, to the tips of Travis's cowboy boots. "I'm embarrassed to admit it, but I was in that disgusting place once. A detective came to my rescue when a rowdy drunk got out of hand. That must have been you."

"Yep. Apparently, I am easy to forget. So why the denials?" Travis asked. "As far as I know, you didn't break any laws that night."

"I absolutely didn't. Not that night or any other. I'd just rather Joni not know I did something so stupid."

"Not only stupid, but dangerous," Travis corrected. "Why were you there?"

"I was writing an article for a magazine on the increase of gentlemen's clubs in the Dallas area. I decided I should at least visit one of them for firsthand research."

"Dressed like that?"

"I thought I'd be less conspicuous that way."

"There was no way you'd ever go unnoticed, looking the way you did that night. Those red shoes alone were enough to guarantee you'd get hit on."

So he'd noticed more than that she'd needed help. At least she'd had an effect on him. Not that she cared.

"I'd love to read that article," Travis said. "Which magazine was that in?"

"It doesn't matter. It was a busy month and they decided not to run the story, after all."

"So all that work for nothing."

"That's freelance," she quipped. Even to her ears the attempt at nonchalance fell flat. She was too nervous. And she'd never written a magazine article in her life. The closest she'd come was a letter to the editor they had actually printed in the newspaper.

"I thought Joni said you worked in the personnel department of a department-store chain."

"Benefits manager, but I occasionally freelance."

"You're a lousy liar."

And always had been. She was going to have to come nearer to the truth if she expected Travis to buy her story.

"Okay, I wasn't there to write an article. A good friend of mine was worried about her daughter. She'd heard a rumor that she was dancing at the Passion Pit. I offered to go there and find out for certain."

"Just helping out a friend."

"Yes. Look, Travis, I know your cop instincts are running wild. But this time they're way off base. I went to a strip club one night. I wasn't looking for a job or trying to pick up tricks. I'm thirty-five years old, for heaven's sake. Way too old to peddle flesh even if I was interested. End of conversation."

"Not quite. If I ever find out that you've exposed my niece to drugs, alcohol or any other sordid behaviors, I'll tell Joni everything and see that you never come around Effie again."

Travis Dalton was not only arrogant, but overbearing. That would have turned her off in a second, except that he was being that way to protect his niece. That was the kind of dogmatism she'd craved from the cops investigating Cornell's disappearance.

The temptation to tell him the truth flared inside her. It passed just as quickly. There was no reason to think he'd be any different than the other officers she'd talked to.

No. She'd made her decision. She had to go higher than the cops if she was to find Cornell. She'd done that. Now she was just waiting to hear back from a man she knew only as Georgio.

"You don't have to worry about Effie," Faith assured him. "I would *never* corrupt a child."

"Good." He opened the door.

She slid past him and climbed behind the wheel. "Good night, Travis."

"One last thing."

She looked up just as he leaned forward. Their faces were mere inches apart. The musky scent of soap, aftershave and sheer manliness attacked her senses, and a riotous surge of attraction made her go weak.

His hand touched her shoulder. "If you ever need to ask me about your friend's problems—if you ever need to talk about anything at all—call me." He reached into his pocket, pulled out a business card and pressed it into her hand.

His voice had lost its threatening edge. His tone was compelling. "I'll do what I can to help, Faith. You can trust me."

Finally, he closed her door. She jerked the car into Reverse, backed from the parking space and then sped away. Her insides were shaking. Tears of frustration burned the back of her eyelids.

Trust him. She'd love nothing more than to believe that. Desperation urged her to turn back. Put Travis Dalton to the test. Avoid getting involved with Georgio, a man whose power frightened her and whose dark and forbidden world made her sick to her stomach.

But she'd tried working with the cops first, lost months doing things their way, wasted precious time not knowing if Cornell was sick, in pain, held captive or even...

No. Cornell was alive. She'd find him. She was on the right track now. Trusting Travis would accomplish nothing except to drag Joni into this nightmare.

Far better if she never saw Travis Dalton again, never gave him another chance to mess with her mind or her resolve.

TRAVIS TOOK A few steps, escaping the cloud of dust Faith left behind in her haste to get away from him. He was one of the best interrogators in the whole homicide department. He could recognize a liar as easily as some people could recognize a guy was bald or a woman was wearing a wig.

And that was with a good liar. Faith Ashburn wasn't. But he still couldn't buy that she was a hooker or an addict looking for a way to feed her demon. So what had she been doing at the Passion Pit that night and what really haunted those captivating deep brown eyes?

Travis started back to the party. He'd lost the mood for celebrating, but he couldn't haul ass without letting Leif know he was leaving. His boots stirred up loose gravel as he neared the sprawling ranch house. Music from the band wafted through the night, competing with the cacophony of thousands of tree frogs, crickets and the occasional howl of a coyote.

Welcoming lights spilled out from every window of the old ranch house. The glow did nothing to make Travis feel more at home, but oddly, he didn't experience any rancor toward the house or the ranch.

Even more surprising, he didn't hate R.J., not the way Leif had at first or the way Travis had expected to before he'd met the man. Hard to hate a dying man, even a father who hadn't bothered to find out if you were dead or alive or being daily abused after your mother died of cancer.

Not hating R.J. didn't mean Travis gave a damn about him or wanted anything to do with him or the bait R.J. was casting out to lure his estranged family home.

Bottom line: if home was where the heart was, the Dry Gulch Ranch didn't make the cut for Travis.

He spotted R.J. rounding the side of the house. The old man hesitated, then swayed as if he was losing his balance. Travis rushed over and caught him just as he started to crumple to the hard earth.

R.J. looked up at him, but his expression was blank and he looked pasty and dazed.

Travis kept a steadying arm around his waist. "Do you need an ambulance?"

R.J. raked his fingers through his thinning gray hair and looked up at Travis. "An ambulance?"

"You almost passed out there."

"Where's Gwen?"

It was the first Travis had heard of a Gwen. "Why don't I get you back inside and I'll see if I can find her?"

R.J. muttered a string of curses. "Just get Gwen. And tell everyone else to go home. Don't know what the hell all these people are doing here, anyway."

His words were slurred, difficult to understand. There was no smell of alcohol on his breath, so Travis figured this had to be related to the tumor.

Leif said R.J. had occasional moments when he wasn't fully lucid, but he hadn't indicated R.J. totally lost it like this. Could be the tumor had shifted or increased in size.

Travis looked around, hoping to see someone who knew more about R.J. than he did heading back to the house or to their car. No such luck. Everyone was obviously still in the party tent.

"Let's go inside," Travis said again. "Maybe Gwen's in there."

He began leading the old man toward the back porch. "Just a few yards to go," Travis said. He walked slowly, supporting most of R.J.'s weight. When they reached the steps, R.J. grabbed hold of the railing.

"Take a second to catch your breath," Travis told him.

R.J. shook his head, then straightened, still a bit shaky. He looked back toward the area where the reception was going full blast and then up at Travis, as if trying to figure out what the devil was going on.

"Did I drag you away from the party?" he asked.

"Nope," Travis said. "I walked someone to their car and ran into you a few yards from the house. You looked like you could use some help."

R.J. scratched his chin. "Damned tumor. Can't make up its mind if it wants to kill me or drive me crazy. Gets me so mixed-up I don't know if I'm shucking or shelling."

"Do you want me to drive you to the emergency room?"

"Hell no. Nothing they can do. I'll just go inside and sit down awhile. Tell Leif that if you see him. I don't want him worrying about what happened to me while he should be celebrating."

"Shouldn't I get someone to come stay with you? You probably shouldn't be alone."

"Nope. Tumor's going to kill me and that's a fact, but it ain't gonna rule me. I'm okay now. You go back to the party afore that looker friend of Joni's you were dancing with hooks up with some other guy."

So the old man didn't miss much when he was lucid. "If you're talking about Faith Ashburn, she's already left."

Probably to hook up with another guy. Hopefully not one picked up anywhere near the Passion Pit.

"C'mon. I'll walk inside with you—not that I think you need help," he added before R.J. could rebuke him. "I could use a glass of water. Then I'll let Leif know where you are and see if I can find Gwen for you."

"Gwen?"

"You mentioned her a minute ago."

"Did I?"

"You did."

"Don't that just stitch your britches? Far as I know, there ain't no Gwen around these parts."

But there had been one wherever R.J. had gone in his mind. By the time they were inside the house, the old man seemed as alert as he had at the start of the evening. He walked on his own to the kitchen, opened the fridge and took out a bottle of milk. Travis reached into the cabinet, took out a glass and set it on the counter for him.

"Join me in a drink?" R.J. asked. "There's beer or whiskey around here somewhere or you can just get water out of the faucet. We don't drink that fancy bottled designer H_2O around here."

Sitting around drinking like old friends with R.J. had about as much appeal as being invited to shovel manure out of the horse barn.

"Another time," Travis said. "If you're okay, I need to be going."

"Sure. I'm good. You head on back to the party. You know your being here tonight meant a lot to your brother."

"I wouldn't have missed it. Leif's family." All the family he had. Meeting R.J. hadn't changed that. "You take care," Travis said. Eager to clear out before the man started talking family or brought up his bizarre will, he turned and started back to the party.

"Thanks, son," R.J. called after him.

Travis didn't stop or turn around. But the word *son* clattered in his head, knocking loose some bad memories as he pulled the front door shut behind him. Memories he'd banished to the deepest, darkest abyss of his mind years ago and wasn't about to let R.J. rekindle.

But Travis had accomplished one thing tonight other than doing his duty by Leif. He now knew the mystery woman from the Passion Pit's name.

First thing tomorrow, he'd start his own investigation of Faith Ashburn—which might plunge him into a new set of problems.

If he discovered that she wasn't as innocent as his hunch indicated and she was involved in some kind of criminal behavior, he'd have no choice but to arrest her.

News that your brother had just arrested your wife's maid of honor would no doubt ensure a dynamic beginning to the honeymoon. Leif would love him for that.

FAITH PULLED ON the cotton T-shirt, drew her bare feet onto the bed and slipped between the crisp sheets. The once-cozy home felt even lonelier than usual tonight.

Perhaps it was the contrast between the glorious future filled with love and happiness stretching in front of Joni and Leif, and the heartbreak that filled these walls that made the desperation almost too much to endure.

Whatever the reason, the fear for Cornell pressed against her chest with such force she could barely breathe. Tales of past real-life abduction horrors roamed her mind like bands of deadly marauders. Victims kept against their will, sometimes for years. Abused. Tortured. Killed.

She shuddered and beat a fist into the pillow. Knowing she'd never find a shred of peace on her own, she finally gave up and retrieved the bottle of antianxiety medication the doctor had prescribed.

She shook two pills from the bottle and swallowed them with a few sips from the glass of water she'd placed on her nightstand earlier. She switched off the lamp and lay in the muted moonlight that filtered through her window. The branches of the oak outside creaked in the wind and sent eerie shadows creeping across her ceiling.

Counting backward, she tried to force her mind to dull and welcome sleep. Instead, her thoughts shifted to Travis. The instant attraction she'd felt in his arms was difficult to figure. Not that his rugged good looks wouldn't have been enough to grab almost any woman's attention, especially one who hadn't been with a man in over two years.

Only it was more what she sensed with him than what she saw. Strength. Determination. Protectiveness toward his niece.

And a promise that she could trust him. She'd wanted to believe that, wanted it so badly that she'd almost turned around and driven back to the ranch after fifteen minutes on the road.

But she'd tried the police. They saw things in black-and-white. Her son had left home. His friends had suggested he was on drugs. He'd been seen in the seedy area of town and inside a strip club where he'd appeared to be enjoying himself.

Their deduction: no foul play suspected.

The police might be right to a point, but she knew her son. He might have caved in to peer pressure and smoked a joint, but he was not an addict. He might even have gone along with friends for a night of carousing, but unless something terrible had happened, he would have come home.

The black of night had eased into the gray of dawn before sleep finally claimed her.

She woke to the jarring ring of the phone. Anticipation stabbed her heart the way it did at every unexpected call, and she grabbed the receiver, knocking over the glass of water. The liquid splattered her arm and the side of her bed as she clutched the phone and put it to her ear.

"Hello."

"Mom."

Chapter Three

Faith's heart pounded against her chest. Her breath caught. She jerked to a sitting position and forced her words through a choking knot at the back of her throat.

"Cornell. Is that you? Is it really you?"

"It's me."

"Where are you? Are you okay?"

"I'm okay. Only…"

"Tell me where you are, Cornell. I'll come get you. Just tell me where you are?"

"I can't, Mom."

"Are you having seizures? Have you been taking your meds?"

"I have a new prescription. No seizures in months." His voice shook. "I'm so sorry. So sor—"

His voice grew silent. Curses railed in the background. The phone went dead.

"Cornell! Cornell!" She kept calling, but she was yelling his name into a lifeless phone. Her insides rolled sickeningly.

"Please call me back. Please, Cornell, call me back," she whispered. The phone stayed silent.

There had to be a way to reach him. A hard metal taste filled the back of her throat as she punched in *69.

A brief sputter of interference was the only response to her attempt to reach the number Cornell had called from.

Her head felt as if someone had turned on strobe lights inside it. A pulsing at the temples tightened like a Vise-Grip. She buried her head in her hands in an attempt to stop the dizzying sensation.

Was this just another nightmare or had she actually heard her son's voice?

No, even trapped in the shock, she was certain the call had been real. Tears burned in the corners of her eyes and then escaped to stream down her face.

Cornell was alive. Finally, the truth of that rolled over her in waves. Her son was alive.

But where was he and what could he possibly be sorry for? For taking drugs? For drinking? Was he staying away because he thought she was mad at him? But if that was all there was, who had yelled the curses in the background that had frightened Cornell into breaking off the call midsentence?

He was not alone and whoever was with had him under their control.

Possibilities exploded in her mind, all of them too frightening to bear.

There had to be a way to find out where that call had originated. If she knew where Cornell was, she could rescue him. She could bring him home.

His interrupted call was proof he was being held or at least intimidated by someone. Even the Dallas Police Department couldn't deny that.

Call me. You can trust me.

Travis's words echoed in her mind. But was it Travis Dalton she should put her faith in or a man she knew only as Georgio?

OFFICIALLY, IT WAS Travis's day off. Unofficially, he strolled into the precinct about 7:00 a.m. No one in the front office seemed surprised to see him. Homicide detectives never kept normal hours.

Neither did crime.

Jewel Sayer raised one eyebrow as he passed her desk. "I thought you were partying in Oak Grove this weekend?"

"Just stayed long enough to get my brother married."

"What? No hot chicks at the wedding reception?"

"None as hot as you, Jewel."

"Can't go comparing the rest of the mere mortals to me, Travis. You've got to learn to settle for someone in your league."

"So you keep telling me."

Jewel was in her mid-thirties and a far cry from the beauty-pageant types who filled the Dallas hot spots six nights a week. She had a boxlike face hemmed in by dark, straight hair cropped an inch from her scalp. Her breasts were lost beneath boxy, plain cotton shirts. Her trousers bagged. Her face was a makeup-free zone.

Jewel was, however, a wildcat of a homicide detective. She could tear more much meat out of a seemingly useless clue than most of the men who'd had years more experience. And she had great instincts. She also had a husband who adored her.

Her phone rang. She lifted her coffee mug as a sign of dismissal before answering it.

Travis stopped at the coffeepot, filled a mug with the strong brew and took it to his office. He dropped to the seat behind his cluttered desk and typed *Faith Ashburn* into the DPD search system.

A few sips of coffee later, her name came up as having filed a missing-person report a few days under ten months ago, on June 25. That would have been approximately six months before he ran into her at the Passion Pit.

He pulled up the report she'd filled out. The missing person was her eighteen-year-old son, Cornell Keating Ashburn, a high-school student about to start his senior year.

According to the report, Cornell struggled with academics and received special help with his classes in a mainstream setting. He made friends easily but he was easily influenced by his peers. He was also on medication for seizures and reportedly needed daily meds to prevent them.

According to the report, Faith Ashburn had gone in to work early the day he'd gone missing, leaving before Cornell got out of bed. She'd come home from work to find a note from him saying he was hanging out with some friends from the neighborhood. He might spend the night at his friend Jason's, but he'd call later and let her know.

He'd never called. He'd never come home. He'd never showed up at Jason's.

That explained the torment that haunted her mesmerizing eyes.

Now that Travis thought about it, Leif had questioned him a couple months ago about how effective the police were with following up on missing-persons cases. Travis had assured him that they were thorough and professional.

No doubt Joni had told him about Faith's missing son and that had prompted the questions.

Travis printed the original report and a series of followup notes by the investigating detective, Mark Ethridge. Mark headed up the missing-persons division and reportedly had handled Cornell's disappearance himself. Ethridge was one of the best in the business at tracking missing or runaway teens.

Travis skimmed for the most pertinent details. Faith and Cornell's father were divorced. He'd died two years ago in a work-related accident, so that eliminated any chance he'd run away to live with him. His maternal grandmother lived in Seattle. His maternal grandfather lived in Waco. Neither had seen Cornell in years. Nor had his paternal grandparents. Ethridge had checked that out thoroughly.

Faith had called everyone Cornell ever hung out with. No one had seen him that day.

His clothes were still in the closet except for the jeans, shirt and sneakers he'd obviously been wearing when he went missing. His iPad and computer were still in his room. Only his phone was missing. She'd called it repeatedly. There had been no answer.

Easy to see why she feared foul play.

Of course, it was also possible the young man had decided to chuck it all and run away from home. At eighteen, he wouldn't technically be a runaway. In the eyes of the law, he was an adult with the right to live wherever he chose.

Travis finished off his coffee and then moved on to the notes Ethridge had provided. There was no final report, as the investigation was ongoing.

Not good, Travis decided as he delved into the investigation discoveries. Although Faith had insisted that her son had no issues that would cause him to run away, his friends from school painted a different story.

Several of his classmates, including Jason, had said he'd started acting strange in the days before he'd disappeared. They said he'd stopped hanging out with them after school, always said he was busy.

Ethridge had checked out the local drug and prostitute scene. Two strippers from the Passion Pit had recognized him from his picture, said they'd seen him in the club a couple times over the past few weeks, but not since his disappearance. One claimed he was hot for one of the dancers.

Even Georgio admitted to having seen him. Said he'd caught Cornell trying to touch one of his dancers inappropriately, and kicked him out. Claimed he realized then the kid was underage, and had told him to go home before he got into trouble.

After that, the clues ran dry.

Ethridge would have told Faith what he'd discovered. That explained her hanging out in the city's scummiest dive. She'd been looking for her son or someone who could tell her where to find him.

The only good news was that Cornell's body had not turned up at the local morgue.

That was the reality Travis lived with every day. He and his partner were the lead detectives in five unsolved murder cases of male victims between the ages of sixteen and eighteen who'd been killed over the past nineteen months. All had been shot twice in the back of the head, gangster-style, their bodies either left in an alley or dumped into the Trinity River.

At first people had paid little attention to the murders, attributing them to gangs or drug deals gone bad. But the last victim had been from a prominent family.

Now the media had jumped on board and were suddenly clamoring for information about the murders and pushing the idea that a serial killer was stalking Dallas.

Nothing got the citizens more riled and afraid than the possibility of a serial killer who chose his victims randomly.

Neither Travis nor his partner, Reno Vargas, believed the murders were random. In fact, they were convinced Georgio was behind them. What they didn't have was proof of his involvement.

Any way you looked at it, Faith Ashburn had plenty of reason to be worried.

Travis was about to go for more coffee when his cell phone vibrated. He yanked it from his pocket and checked the caller ID. Faith Ashburn's name lit up the display.

He glanced at his watch. Only seven thirty-five and on a Sunday morning. He'd hoped he might hear from her, but he definitely hadn't expected her to call this soon. He doubted it was personal, which meant she was calling about Cornell.

"Detective Travis Dalton," he answered. "What can I do for you?"

"Travis, this is Faith."

He liked the way she said his name. He didn't like the tremor of apprehension in her voice. "Hi, Faith. Nice to hear from you."

"It's…" She paused. "I need to talk to you, as a detective. It's about my son."

"Cornell?"

"You know about his disappearance?"

"I didn't until a few minutes ago. I just finished reading the missing-person report."

"There's a new development," she said.

"Since last night?"

"Yes."

"What kind of development?"

"I'd rather not talk about it over the phone. Actually, I suppose I should call Mark Ethridge, but I'm not even sure he's kept the investigation open, and you did offer to help."

"Don't worry about the chain of command. I'll handle that. I was going to talk to Ethridge about the case, anyway. When do you want to get together?"

"As soon as possible."

"Right now works for me. How about breakfast?"

"That would be great. I can meet you anywhere you say."

"I'm almost finished up here, so how about I pick you up at your place?"

"What time?"

He reached for the form she'd filled out, and checked her home address. It was probably a twenty-minute drive in light Sunday-morning traffic. "Is a half hour from now too soon?"

"That would be perfect, but, Travis..." She paused again. Unsure of him or facing new fears? He couldn't tell which.

"Go on," he urged.

"Don't mention to Joni or Leif that I called you."

"Joni surely knows your son is missing."

"Yes. They both do. Leif even offered to hire a private detective to help find him."

"You turned him down?"

"I'd already hired one."

That, Travis hadn't known. "Your decision," he said. "You don't have to admit to anyone you called me, if that's how you want it."

"It's just that I don't want to spoil Joni and Leif's honeymoon, and there's nothing either of them can do.

Besides, Joni has spent enough time holding my hand and crying with me over the last ten months."

"Then this is our secret," he said. "See you in half an hour. I'll try to offer more than a hand or a shoulder to cry on—though I have both if they're needed."

"Just help me find Cornell and bring him home."

Travis couldn't promise to bring him home. Cornell would have a say in that. But he would find him. Hopefully, alive.

He left the precinct and headed to her house. She lived in a neighborhood of small brick homes built close together, with well-tended yards. No gated access. Few trees. Driveways sported basketball hoops.

A young man pushed a baby stroller down the narrow sidewalk. An attractive woman in white shorts and a knit shirt walked behind them, keeping a close watch on a toddler who was pedaling furiously on her bright red trike.

It looked to be a good middle-class neighborhood to grow up in. Much nicer than the one Travis had lived in for the first few years after his mother's death.

Then, most of the houses had been in need of repair and drive-by shootings were as commonplace as his foster father's drunken binges.

Travis figured if it hadn't been for his mother's influence during the early years and Leif's efforts to rescue him from the ghetto, he might have grown up as troubled and in trouble as the young punks who committed most of the crimes in Dallas.

He turned at the corner and started checking addresses. Faith's house was in the middle of the block, a redbrick with white trim. The hedges were neatly groomed. Colorful pansies and snapdragons overflowed from pots by her door. In spite of her grief, she was keeping up appearances. Probably wanted home to be welcoming if or when Cornell showed up again.

Travis pulled into the driveway and took the walk to her covered entry. She opened the door seconds after he pushed the bell, handbag in hand, clearly ready to go.

"You're prompt," she said, stepping out the door without inviting him in.

"Also loyal, and I floss after every meal."

A quick smile played on her lips but didn't penetrate the veil of apprehension that covered her eyes.

She walked in front of him to his car. The white jean shorts she wore were cuffed at mid-thigh. Not too tight, but fitted enough to accentuate the sway of her hips. A teal blouse tied at the waist. The morning sun painted golden highlights in her dark hair.

He had to hurry to reach the door and open it for her before she climbed in on her own. He got a whiff of her flowery perfume as she slid past him. Crazy urges bucked around inside him. Not the time or the place, he reminded himself. Business only—at least until Cornell was found.

"There's a breakfast spot in a strip center just a few blocks from here," Faith said. "I hear they have good pancakes."

"Do you like pancakes?" he asked.

"I used to, when I was a kid. I usually just have toast and coffee for breakfast now. I doubt my stomach will even tolerate that this morning."

"No appetite, huh? Is that because of the new development you're going to tell me about?"

She nodded, and he thought again how youthful she looked to be the mother of a teenager. She'd said she was thirty-five, which meant she'd given birth to him at seventeen. There must be a story there, as well.

"Tell me where to go," he said.

He followed her directions. The restaurant was small, noisy and crowded. Not the best spot for a serious conversation."

"Any chance we can get a seat on the patio?" he asked the young blonde hostess.

"How many in your party?"

"Two."

"I think I can manage that."

She smiled and led them to a table in the middle of the patio.

"How about that table in the back?" he asked.

"Okay with me, but it doesn't have an umbrella, so you're going to be in the sun."

But it would give them a lot more privacy. He looked to Faith.

"The sun is fine with me," she said.

Once they were seated, the hostess set two menus in front of them and announced that the waitress would be with them shortly.

"I didn't realize the place would be so noisy," Faith said. "I just need to talk and this was the closest café I could think of."

Her apprehension seemed to be growing. He scooted his menu aside. "Let's hear it. I can't do anything about solving the problem until I know what it is."

She clasped her hands in front of her. "I got a phone call from Cornell just before daybreak this morning."

Travis hadn't seen that coming. Even if he had, he would have expected it to be good news. Hearing the kid was alive made him feel a hell of a lot better, and he didn't even know him.

"What did he say?"

"That he was sorry."

"That's a good start. Sorry for what?"

"He didn't say."

"Where is he?"

"I asked, but he didn't answer that, either."

"He must have said something more than 'I'm sorry' to have you this upset."

"It's what he didn't say that has me so afraid, Travis. The call was a cry for help. I have to find out where he was when he made that call. That's why I came to you."

The waitress appeared at their elbow. "Are you ready to order?"

"Just coffee for now," Travis said. "Black."

"Same for me," Faith said, "except I'll need cream and an artificial sweetener."

"Something got lost in translation," Travis said as the waitress walked away. "The dots between 'I'm sorry' and the call being a cry for help don't connect for me. Start at the beginning and tell me exactly what was said."

The waitress returned with their coffee. Faith stirred in the cream and sweetener slowly, as if she was trying to get her thoughts together. Finally, she looked up and locked her gaze with his.

"'Mom,'" she murmured. "I answered the phone and heard 'Mom.'" She picked up her napkin and used it to dab a tear from the corner of her right eye. More moisture gathered. "At that point I think I went into momentary shock."

In Travis's mind she wasn't far from shock now, just having to relive the moment.

"After ten months of silence, I can see why that jolted you," Travis said.

"So much so that I asked if it was really him."

"You weren't sure from the sound of his voice?"

"Only for a few seconds. My heart was beating so fast

I couldn't think. I thought I might be dreaming. But it was Cornell. I know it was. I'd know his voice anywhere."

"And after he said 'Mom'?"

"I asked him about his seizure meds. He said he'd gotten a prescription and that he was taking them. Then he just said he was sorry."

"For leaving home?"

"He didn't *leave* home." Frustration laced her voice. "At least not of his own accord. He would never do that. I told Detective Ethridge and the private detective I hired that he had no reason to leave home. I don't think either of them ever believed me, but a mother knows her son. At least I know Cornell."

Travis reached across the table and laid his hands on top of hers. "I believe you, Faith. I'm just trying to see the whole picture here so I can get a handle on the situation. It would help if he'd said what he was sorry for."

"He never got the chance to tell me. Someone started yelling curses in the background. Before he could say more, the connection was broken, either by Cornell or by the person who was yelling at him."

"Was the voice in the background male or female?"

"Male. I pushed *69 and tried to redial the number, but it wouldn't come up. I called the phone company. They were no help, either. But you're a homicide detective. You must have ways to get that number."

"Did he call your cell phone or landline?"

"The house phone. I can give you my number."

"I'll need that for starters, but I'd like to take a look around Cornell's room and also check out his computer."

"Arsenio checked the computer thoroughly."

"Arsenio?"

"Arsenio Gomez, the P.I. I hired. He said there was nothing there to lead him to Cornell."

"I'd like to look for myself."

"Of course. Do anything that you think might help us find my son. Please, just do it quickly, before the lead grows cold again."

"I'll do everything I can to help you find Cornell, Faith. But first we need to set a few ground rules."

Faith met his gaze head-on, suspicion arching her brows. "What kind of ground rules?"

"I expect the truth from you, the total truth."

"I have no reason to lie."

"No, but sometimes it's difficult for parents to face up to the truth about their child. If there's any indication that Cornell was on drugs or mixed up with a gang, I need to know that up front. Not to judge him. But it might change the way I go about the investigation."

Faith yanked her hands away from his. Her lips grew taut, her eyes fiery. "I know what you read in his missing-person file, Travis. I know what his friends said about him and that he was seen at the Passion Pit, but Cornell was only eighteen. He may have made some bad decisions. But he wasn't a thug or an addict. He didn't leave home by choice, and wherever he is, he's being held against his will. I'm as sure of that as I am that my name is Faith Ashburn or that today is Sunday."

Travis wasn't convinced, but he did understand her desperation. It was a dangerous world out there. No one knew that better than him.

Which brought up another issue. "There's one other ground rule," Travis said.

"Do you always have so many rules?"

"All depends on the game I find myself in."

"So what's the rule?"

"You leave the investigating to me. No more trips to the Passion Pit or any other questionable location."

"I'm smart enough to know how to avoid trouble."

"I'm questioning your judgment, not your intelligence. I saw you in action, remember? Besides, I have a lot more experience and muscle than you, and I wouldn't go near that dive if I wasn't carrying a weapon."

"If it's that dangerous, why don't the police shut the club down and put Georgio out of business?"

Georgio. Merely hearing his name from her lips made Travis sick. "What do you know about Georgio?"

"Just that he's the owner of the Passion Pit."

"And an offspring of the devil. Stay away from him, Faith. That's an order."

The waitress returned with refills. This time Travis ordered two eggs, over easy, with sausage, grits, biscuits and gravy, without bothering to look at the menu. Faith ordered a slice of wheat toast.

"If you'll give me your home phone number now, I'll make a call and get the ball rolling," Travis said.

She took a pen from her purse and scribbled the number down on a paper napkin. "How long will it take to track the call?"

"Depends on where the call was made from. If luck's on our side, we could have the phone number by the time we finish breakfast."

"In minutes." She sounded almost breathless. "Cornell could be home in time for dinner."

Damn. He should never have gotten her hopes up like that. "Don't count on instant gratification," he cautioned. "Have to take things one step at a time, but if we discover where that call was made from, we'll be one huge leap ahead of where you were when you went to bed last night."

"I'll take that," she said. "But if we find out where he called from, we should be able to find him."

They would have to play this smart. No rushing in without knowing for certain what they were up against. If Cornell was really being held against his will, making a foolish mistake could get him killed.

At this point, the best they could hope for was that Cornell Ashburn had just developed a sudden taste for independence, women and drugs, and taken a leave of absence from home to satisfy his cravings.

He definitely wouldn't be the first eighteen-year-old to sow his wild oats. Travis knew that firsthand.

He put the search for the phone number in motion and then his focus returned to Faith Ashburn. She wasn't beautiful, but she was attractive and natural. Her smile, her eyes, her intensity—it all got to him.

And it was meshing with an overwhelming need to protect her and get to know her better. Maybe it was the wedding thing. Seeing Leif so happy to settle down with one woman could be addling Travis's brain.

If he was smart, he'd turn this back over to Mark Ethridge and run for the hills. But even if he wanted to, he couldn't do that. Not with the possibility that her son's disappearance could in any way be connected to the four others who had gone missing over the past nineteen months and turned up dead. The pressure was on to solve the case before another young man lost his life.

A young man like Cornell.

In spite of his concerns, when the waitress arrived with the food, Travis dived in like a starving man. If he let worry or even murder interfere with his eating, he'd have to go on life support.

He didn't hear back about the origins of Faith's early-morning call during breakfast or on the drive back to her house. Once there, he went straight to Cornell's room and began searching with the same intensity he'd use for a fresh crime scene.

Travis pulled several boxes from the back of the closet. One held a half-dozen pairs of tennis shoes, two jackets that were too heavy for Dallas winters and a pair of hiking boots.

"Cornell loved outdoor activities," Faith said by way of explanation. "Skiing, hiking, white-water rafting, horseback riding. His dad's brother used to own a condo in the Colorado Rockies, and Cornell visited him with his dad several times. He loved it out there, even talked about moving there one day."

"Have you checked with his uncle to see if he was with him?"

"His uncle died in a snowmobile accident three years ago, just a year before Cornell's father was killed while working on an oil rig in the Gulf of Mexico. My son has never fully gotten over those deaths."

"That would be hard on anyone." And it definitely gave Cornell a reason to be troubled. "How old was Cornell when you got divorced?"

"Ten. That's when I met Joni. I needed some job skills, so I went back for an associate degree."

Faith's house phone rang. She gasped and grabbed her chest as she ran to answer it. Travis followed, listening in on the conversation until he was certain Cornell wasn't the caller.

He went back to the boy's room alone to continue the search. All he found was typical teenage stuff. A worn baseball glove. Video games. Old comic books. Some swimming trophies from when he was in grade school.

Nothing that provided even a hint or a clue of where Cornell might have gone or why. Travis had started to put them back in place when he noticed a smaller box pushed to the back of the shelf. He took it down, opened it and peered inside.

A porn magazine stared back at him. He lifted it to find eight more, all with pictures of naked women, nothing sadistic or particularly kinky.

All well hidden from his mother.

No surprise. Guys of eighteen seldom confided those kinds of thoughts and activities to their mothers. But if Travis and Faith were going to find Cornell, they would have to go into this with their eyes wide open.

He stuck his head out the bedroom door. "Faith, want to come in here a minute?"

She arrived a few seconds later, breathless from racing up the stairs. The look on her face was expectant, downright hopeful.

He hated that what he had to show her would replace it with a kick in the gut. He tried to think of something to make this easier on her, but he'd never been great at dancing around the truth.

He set the box on the table. "This might explain why Cornell was spotted at the Passion Pit."

Faith pushed back the cover of the top magazine with one finger, as if was too disgusting to touch. Tough on a mother to find out her baby wasn't one.

Travis's cell phone vibrated. Caller ID indicated it was from the precinct. "I need to take this," he said.

Faith nodded.

His focus quickly switched to the call and the information relayed to him by one of the younger officers recently appointed to serve under him in the homicide division.

The news was not good.

Chapter Four

Travis's find made Faith sick to her stomach. She steadied herself against the bedpost while she tried to put the magazines into perspective.

So he wasn't as innocent and naive as she'd believed. It was only natural he'd have the same physical urges as other boys his age. That still didn't explain his disappearance.

Or the interrupted phone call. Or why he hadn't called back.

But she hated that it had taken ten months to find out that her son had porn hidden in his room. That probably wouldn't have helped her or the police find him. But what else had been going on in his life that she didn't suspect?

Had he grown from a kid to a man without her realizing it? When had she lost touch with him?

Faith looked up, suddenly aware of the gravity in Travis's low, deep-toned voice as he talked on the phone, and wondered if he was talking about Cornell or one of his homicide cases.

She studied the lines and planes of his profile. His face was tanned, his brows as dark as his hair, his face narrowing into a prominent chin and jawline.

He wasn't pretty-boy handsome, but he was definitely the kind of man who'd stand out in a crowd. The archetype of strength and masculinity. His looks and manner instilled confidence. If anyone could find Cornell, it would be Travis Dalton.

Or was it her own desperation that made her read those qualities into him? If so, it was a mistake she couldn't afford to make.

"Disturbing news?" she asked once he'd broken the connection and returned the phone to his pocket.

"Could have been better."

"Does it have to do with Cornell?"

"Afraid so."

A new wave of apprehension flooded though her. "Were they able to trace the call?"

"Yes and no."

"What does that mean?"

"We have a general location, but not a specific one."

"But a general location is better than nothing," she insisted. "It gives us an area to start searching for him."

"A very large and undefined area. The call was made from Texas, somewhere near the Mexican border south of San Antonio. But the phone used to make the call was purchased in Mexico. That places Cornell either north or south of the border."

"Doesn't the phone-service company have an address for the subscriber?"

"It's not registered to a subscriber."

"So it's like one of those phones you can buy at a convenience store with a certain number of minutes included."

"Exactly."

"So all we really know is that Cornell is somewhere near the Mexican border." Terror rumbled inside her. The border towns were known for their violent drug cartels, especially on the Mexico side.

Murders had risen to the point that few Americans ventured into them. Most of the police were rumored to be corrupt or so afraid of the cartels they couldn't do their job. She and Cornell had watched a special about that on TV just last year. He'd been disgusted with the whole idea of criminals running over honest citizens.

"Cornell would never have gone to Mexico on his own," Faith said. She dropped to the side of the bed. "He's been abducted, Travis. I'm more certain of that than ever now. I have to find him, even if it means going into Mexico." Her voice rose with her growing hysteria.

Travis shoved the magazines aside, dropped to the bed beside her. "I know how frightened you are, Faith, but believe me, going down there won't help, and it could put you in danger."

"Then what will help, Travis? Sitting here doing nothing? Endless talking and promises from Mark Ethridge and now you? Waiting to hear that my son has been..."

A shudder ripped through her. Tears burned her eyes and then began to roll down her cheeks.

Travis snaked an arm around her shoulder. She started to push away from him, but the pain overpowered her stubbornness. Impulsively, she dropped her head to his shoulder and submitted to the ragged sobs.

Travis didn't say a word until she'd cried herself out and pulled herself together. Even then, he didn't move his arm from around her shoulder.

She pulled away. Talk. For ten months all the police had given her was talk. Why had she ever thought Travis would be different?

"I have connections in the towns on both sides of the border, Faith. Let me speak with them and put them on alert," Travis pleaded. "They know how to handle this, who to talk to, where to look."

"Then why haven't the police already done that?"

"I'm sure they have, but I'll put on the pressure. Give me forty-eight hours. If we don't have a lead by then, I'll make a trip to the area."

Faith walked to the other side of the room before turning back to him. "Anything could happen in forty-eight hours."

"Anything could have happened in the last ten months," Travis said. "But you heard Cornell's voice. You know he's alive, and he didn't actually tell you he was in danger when he called."

"If he wasn't being held against his will, he'd be home. I don't know why I can't make anyone understand that."

"I'm trying, Faith. Believe me, I'm looking at this from all angles. I'd like to take Cornell's computer with me to see what additional information I can glean from it."

"It's a waste of time. Officer Ethridge and the private investigator I hired have both already checked the computer out and found nothing. Nothing suspicious on his email or any of his social-media pages. And nothing in the websites he'd visited offered so much as one decent lead."

"I'd like to take that a step further," Travis said. "The DPD has one of the best computer forensics experts in the country. He can discover ambient data that the average Joe has no idea exists on the hard drive. He's found critical information to help me solve a murder case more times than I can count."

"What kind of data do you expect to find?"

"It's the unexpected that usually produces the best evidence. I'll see if I can get a rush on this."

Travis's dedication seemed genuine, and if she could believe his rhetoric, he was ready to make finding Cornell a priority. But why? He was a homicide detective. This was way outside his line of duty.

"Why are you taking this on with such fervor, Travis? This isn't your job. It isn't you responsibility."

"Let's just say any friend of my new sister-in-law's is a friend of mine. And from what I hear, you're her best friend, practically family."

"And from what I hear, you don't even claim kin to your own father."

"There is that," Travis admitted. "So I guess we'll have to go with that I'm one of the good guys."

Strangely, she believed him. Yet she wasn't convinced he understood the urgency. All her instincts stressed that the call from Cornell had been a sign that his fear was growing. He'd taken a risk to call her, and someone else had heard him on the phone. They were running out of time.

"You'll let me know immediately if you hear anything at all?" she insisted as they went back downstairs.

"I promise. You do the same. If you hear from Cornell, call me at once."

"I will, and I pray that's tonight."

"Keep that thought." Travis stopped at the foot of the stairs. "I have a few more questions, but I need to get started with what I have, talk to my contacts, call in some favors."

All things that should have been done months before. Instead, Cornell had simply fallen through the cracks. She really wanted to believe it would be different this time, that Travis was as good as his word.

But did she trust him enough to cancel her appointment with Georgio tomorrow? A man like that didn't play by the rules, but he got things done. At least that was the impression she'd gotten anytime his name had come up while she was hanging out in his territory, searching for Cornell.

Travis stepped out the front door. Then, propping his hand against the doorframe, he leaned in close.

Awareness zinged through her. Her response to his nearness was unwelcome, almost frightening. She was thirty-five years old. She'd been married and divorced. Her son was missing and likely in danger. She didn't fall for men she'd just met.

It was just that her nerves were so rattled her emotions couldn't be trusted.

"Remember the ground rules," he warned. "No putting yourself in danger. Leave the investigation up to me."

"Then find my son."

She took a backward step, willing her mind to focus only on Cornell. Still, as she watched Travis turn and saunter down the walk, she couldn't help wondering what it would be like to have his arms around her for something more than to offer comfort.

A DROP OF MAYONNAISE dripped from Faith's cheese sandwich onto the granite countertop. Grabbing a napkin, she dabbed her mouth and then wiped up the spill. Eating dinner while standing at the counter had become a habit since Cornell's disappearance, a way of avoiding the empty feeling of sitting at the table without him.

Faith took another bite of the tasteless sandwich and then crushed it into the napkin and tossed it into the trash. Before Cornell had gone missing, Sunday nights had been her favorite time of the week. She and Cornell had initiated it as family night right after the divorce, and with few exceptions, they always spent it together.

They'd order in a pepperoni pizza—Cornell's favorite—and wash it down with icy glasses of root beer as they watched a movie in the family room. Most of the time Cornell picked the flick, so in recent years there had been no shortage of car chases, explosions, villains and heroes. Not Faith's genre of choice, but relaxing with Cornell had been worth enduring the gore.

Her phone rang. Hope sent a jolt to her heart, making it bounce off the walls of her chest. She grabbed the phone.

"Hello."

"Hi. It's me, Joni."

Faith swallowed the disappointment and tried to keep her tone light. "You're on your honeymoon. What are you doing wasting your time calling me?"

"I just wanted to say thanks again for being my maid of honor last night."

"You're welcome. It was a beautiful wedding."

"It was. I feel so lucky to be part of the Dalton clan. As soon as we get our house finished, you'll have to come out and stay a few days."

"Sure. I'd like that. But you didn't have to call and tell me that from your honeymoon, not with that gorgeous hunk you're married to."

"Actually, that's not the only reason I called. I wanted to make sure you're all right."

"Why wouldn't I...?" Her mind answered the question before she finished asking it. "You must have talked to Travis."

"He called Leif. He said he was going to help you find Cornell."

"Is that all he told him?"

"Is there more?"

Joni was already worried about her. There was no point in lying. "I had a phone call from Cornell this morning."

"That's great news. You must be so relieved to know he's alive and safe."

"I know he's alive. I don't' know that he's safe. If he wasn't being held against his will, he wouldn't have just called and said nothing. He'd be home."

"Travis said you took the call as a cry for help."

"How else can I take it? You know Cornell, Joni. You know how close we were."

"I do know, Faith. That's why I called. I was hoping to reassure you."

"How can you, unless Travis told Leif something he hasn't told me?"

"I only know what Leif told me. He said Travis is committed to finding Cornell. And according to Leif, once Travis makes up his mind to do something, you can consider it done. I thought it might help if you heard that."

"Thanks."

"So trust him, Faith. Get some sleep tonight and try not to worry."

"I'll try."

Leif's confidence in his brother was reassuring, but even as she finished the conversation with Joni and broke the connection, Faith knew she'd never have a moment's peace until she was face-to-face with her missing son and could see that he was unharmed.

That was why at noon tomorrow, she'd make her way to the Passion Pit. She'd ignore Travis's ground rules and keep her appointment with a mysterious man from the dangerous underbelly of the city.

She'd do whatever she had to do to find her son—inside or outside the law.

Chapter Five

Cornell turned the water as hot as it would go, picked up the bar of soap and rubbed his hands vigorously. Staring at the drain as the bubbles spun into the pipes, he felt the memories hit again.

The liquid instantly changed from clear to a bright crimson. His hands were sticky. His throat was so dry he couldn't swallow. He took deep breaths, trying to keep from throwing up into the sink and having the vomit mix with the blood. Sickeningly, the way it had done that first morning after the murder.

The room began to spin and he closed his eyes and clutched the edge of the stained sink to keep from falling. Finally, the horrifying sensations passed.

When Cornell opened his eyes again, it was only water spraying over his fingers to disappear down the drain. He turned off the faucet, grabbed the worn, faded towel and dried his hands.

"You okay?" Tom Snyder asked as Cornell walked out of the bathroom. "You're not about to have one of those seizures, are you?"

He shrugged. "What if I do?"

"I don't like 'em. They freak me out."

"*You* don't like them?" Cornell muttered a few curse words that he'd never have uttered around his mother.

Not that he got any thrill out of cussing. When it was all you ever heard, it got to be habit. "What the hell do you think they do for me?"

"Obviously make you insane."

"Well, they never did before. Anyway, I'm not having a seizure."

"Good. But no more stupid stunts like calling your mother. Georgio would throw you to the wolves if he knew about that."

"Don't worry. I won't make that mistake again." But not for the reasons Tom was talking about. Hearing his mother's voice had done strange things to Cornell's thinking. Made him so homesick that it was all he could do not to cry. Made him ache to open up and tell his mother everything.

But what would that do except destroy her? She'd try to love him the way she always had, but how could she once she knew what he'd done? And in the end, there was nothing she could do to change any of it.

"Want to go out and get a margarita?" Tom asked. "Looks like we're gonna be stuck here for another night. Might even get a little action, if you know what I mean."

Cornell knew what he meant. "You go ahead. I think I'm going to hit the sack early tonight."

"Man, if you get any more boring, even the cockroaches are going to quit hanging around."

"I can live with that."

"Suit yourself."

Cornell could live without the cockroaches, but he wasn't sure how much longer he could live with Tom and having no control over his life. He couldn't go home, but that didn't mean he had to do slave duty for Georgio for the rest of his days.

Not if things worked out the way he planned.

Chapter Six

Faith parked her car at approximately a quarter hour before her noon appointment with Georgio. This time she was dressed comfortably in black slacks and a white blouse. The turquoise cardigan she had thrown over her shoulders was not for the weather, which had turned quite warm, but because people in Dallas tended to keep their air-conditioning blasting from the first sign of spring well into October.

She looked around as she got out of the car. It was a fairly safe area in spite of the bars and clubs that were on almost every corner. Someone had told her once that it was because Georgio was the law around here and trouble was bad for business. All she knew was that he was a hard man to get to talk to—unless he decided he wanted to deal with you.

It was an old section of town, a mix of decaying residential structures and businesses that were struggling or out of business. Many of those had boarded-up windows and were decorated with fading graffiti.

Two elderly ladies were checking out baskets of fresh produce set just outside the front door of a mom-and-pop grocery store. A few adolescent boys were recklessly darting through traffic on their skateboards. One man shook his fist out his car window and yelled at them to get out of the way. They laughed and kept going.

Three elderly men sat on a bench in front of the barbershop, chatting. An overweight woman with frizzled brown hair was sweeping the walk in front of a hair and nail salon. She looked up and smiled, the lines around her eyes crinkling as Faith hurried past.

Faith hesitated at the double doors to the Passion Pit and then pushed through them, head high. No more pretending she had any business in this establishment except finding her son.

An attractive blonde in tight-fitting black shorts and a scrap of top that covered little more than her nipples greeted her.

"I'm here to see Georgio," Faith said.

The hostess barely glanced at her before tossing her hair and studying the glittery red polish on her long nails as if she was totally bored. "If you're looking for a job, you'll have to talk to Laney. He does all the hiring, but he won't be here until after four."

"I'm not looking for work. My name is Faith Ashburn. I have an appointment with Georgio," she said firmly.

"In that case, wait here and I'll see if he's available."

He'd better be available. If he wasn't, Faith would stage a sit-in at his office door until he was. No way was she going to be given the runaround today, the way she had been for the past ten months.

The first time she'd tried to talk to Georgio—before she knew anything about him except that he was the owner of the club where Cornell had been spotted before his disappearance—she'd just walked up to him one night and started asking questions.

Okay, accosted him and accused him of luring underage kids into his depraved establishment. She'd stuck

Cornell's picture in his face and demanded to know if he'd seen her son.

His bulging-muscled bodyguards took over from there, appearing like attack dogs called to defend. They'd escorted her to the door and forbade her to return, with threats of arrest and prosecution.

Another reason she'd started dressing in full slut regalia whenever she went searching for Cornell.

But that hadn't stopped her from trying to get in touch with Georgio. She'd called at least a dozen times to request the opportunity to talk to him about her son. She'd never gotten past his assistant, Laney, who'd been no help at all.

But today was different. This time Georgio had initiated their visit. Apparently, he'd finally noticed the flyers she was continuously posting around the neighborhood, and had mentally paired Cornell's last name with that of the woman whose calls he'd been ignoring for months.

Hopefully, some of her hard work was finally going to pay off.

Faith followed the hostess down a narrow hallway with a multitude of doors, mostly closed. At the end of it, the seductive young woman tapped on one and announced that Faith was here.

"Show her in."

The voice was deep. The broad-shouldered, well-dressed man who looked her up and down as she entered his office was younger than she'd remembered—early fifties or thereabouts. He was no less intimidating, even without his bodyguards.

She took a deep breath and stared him down. Cornell's life was at stake. She wouldn't be bullied into not going through with this.

"Have a seat, Ms. Ashburn." Georgio motioned to the

leather chair near his desk. She sat, crossing her legs and taking in the expensive furnishings. There was no doubt about his financial success. The hostess left them alone, closing the door behind her.

Georgio continued to stand for a few seconds, towering above the massive desk. He was several inches over six feet tall, with thick salt-and-pepper hair, neatly coiffed. He wasn't bad looking, but his square face and dominating jawline gave him a tough ruffian look in spite of his impressive suit and tie.

When he finally sat down, he leaned back in his chair and smiled. "What can I help you with, Ms. Ashburn?"

She had an idea that he knew exactly why she was here. He didn't seem like a man who liked surprises.

"My son, Cornell Ashburn, is missing," she said, the tremble returning to her voice the way it always did when she was forced to say the dreaded words out loud.

"So you must be responsible for the many flyers I've noticed in the area."

"Yes. I'm glad someone's seen them. They seem to disappear as soon as I put them up. I'm offering a twenty-five-thousand-dollar reward for information leading me to him." The total amount left in her savings account.

Georgio propped his fingertips together and let his penetrating stare lock with hers. "Then I'd be surprised to learn you're not getting a few calls."

"Not even one."

"I'm sorry to hear that. Have the police had better luck?"

"Not much. Nor did the private detective I hired. You're my last hope."

His brows arched. "Exactly how is it you think I can be of service?"

"The Passion Pit is one of the last places my son was seen before he disappeared."

"Really? Was he here with friends?"

"No. Apparently he was here alone."

"And you say he came in here before he went missing?"

"Yes, but only a few nights before."

"Do you know that for a fact?"

"The police questioned you and showed you his picture. You told them that you'd seen him in here yourself on at least two different occasions. One of your dancers also recognized him, only she said he'd been a regular over the last few months."

"How long ago was that?"

"Ten months."

Georgio's face registered surprise. "No wonder I don't remember. I own not only the Passion Pit but two other gentlemen's clubs as well, both busier and more impressive than this one. A lot of young men have walked through my doors since then."

"But surely not all of them went missing."

"Why did you wait so long to come talk to me?" Georgio asked.

"I didn't." She tried unsuccessfully to hide her irritation. "I've called countless times. You either ignored the messages I left or decided not to see me."

Faith pulled Cornell's picture from the side pocket of her handbag and handed it to him. "This is my son's yearbook picture from last year. It was taken several months before he disappeared. It's the same picture the police showed you."

Georgio studied the photo. "Nice clean-cut young man, but if he was in high school, he was too young to be hanging out at the Passion Pit. He would never have gotten past the front door."

"He shouldn't have, but he did. You told Detective Ethridge you realized he was underage and kicked him out."

"We follow policy." He dropped the picture to the desk. "I wish I could help you, Ms. Ashburn, but I haven't seen your son around the club. But if I do, I'll definitely give you a call. How old is he?"

"Eighteen. I know what you're thinking. But he didn't just choose to move out. Cornell's not like that. He's…"

The words caught in her throat. When she tried to tell people about Cornell, she made him sound weak and nerdy. But that wasn't it.

She took a deep breath. "I know my son. He would never have just left and shut me out of his life."

"So you think he met with foul play?"

"Yes. I'm convinced of it, more than ever since the phone call."

Georgio leaned forward, showing the first traces of concern. "Cornell called you?"

She fed him the details as succinctly as possible.

"I can certainly understand your worry, Faith. May I call you Faith?"

"Please do." Especially if that meant he was warming up to her and considering offering his help.

Georgio stood and walked to the front of the desk, leaning back against it so that he was looking directly at her. "I can see how upset you are, but what makes you think I can do more than the police have done?"

"You don't have to keep to the strictures of the law."

A satisfied smile crossed his lips, as if she'd paid him a compliment. If it took flattery to bring him around, she could dish it out.

"I know you're a rich and powerful man with many

contacts," she said, feeding his ego. "If anyone can help me find Cornell and bring him home safely, I think it's you."

"I'm not sure how you reached that conclusion, but I'll tell you what, Faith. I like you and I can tell you're worried sick. I can't make any promises, but I'll see what I can find out."

Her pulse began to race. All these months of searching with little real progress, and now both Travis and Georgio were offering their help. That had to be a good sign.

"Time is of the essence," she urged.

"Okay, but don't go expecting miracles, Faith."

"I have to. If I didn't, I'd never be able to keep going."

Georgio nodded. "Then we'll see what we can do. But there is one thing you should know."

"What's that?"

"I run an honest business here and in my other Dallas nightclubs as well, but I don't work with the police."

"Why is that?"

"Let's just say they don't appreciate some of the finer points of my business. If I'm going to help you find your son, let's keep them off the radar. Don't mention to anyone with the Dallas Police Department that you've even talked to me."

"If that's the way you want it."

"It's the way I insist it be."

That should be easy enough, since Travis had warned her to stay away from Georgio.

"This is between you and me," she promised. "When can you start?"

He smiled. "You do get down to business. I like that. I'll make some calls today, see what I can dig up."

"Is there anything else you'll need from me?"

"Perhaps. But not yet." He picked up the photo again. "May I keep this?"

"Absolutely."

His desk phone rang. "Excuse me for a minute." He punched a button on the receiver and took the call. From his end of the conversation she could tell that he didn't like what he was hearing.

"Something's come up that requires my immediate attention," he told her when he'd finished. "But I have your number and I'll get back with you soon."

"I'll be waiting for your call." That was the understatement of the century. She let herself out and started down the long hallway.

She couldn't deny the relief that his promise of help had stirred, but her nerves were still on edge. Travis had been specific. She was to stay away from Georgio and the Passion Pit and let him handle this.

If it came down to which of the two men she trusted more, it was definitely Travis. But he was a cop. Georgio was an inside man. She needed them both and couldn't afford to turn down any offer of help. Travis should understand that.

She picked up her pace, eager to get back into the sunshine and grab a cup of coffee before going to her office. Her boss had been extremely understanding over the past months, but they were shorthanded this week and she had to carry her load.

She rummaged in her handbag for her keys as she walked. She could hear the music coming from the club now, and footfalls and low voices.

Travis's voice. Her heart pounded. She stopped dead still and listened. What would he be doing here in the middle of the day on a Monday?

But it was him, apparently just around the corner and

walking toward her. She so did not need this. At the last second, she ducked into an open doorway and pulled the door closed behind her.

She barely breathed until she heard him pass. From the sound of the footsteps and voices, she guessed he was with another detective.

Were they here to question Georgio about Cornell or as part of a homicide investigation? Was Georgio in some kind of trouble? Was that why he wanted nothing to do with the police? Whatever the reason, he had clearly been irritated at their arrival.

She waited until the voices and footsteps had faded into the distance before cracking the door enough to peek out and see into the hall. There was no sign of Travis. Her insides rolled as she slipped out of the room and walked as fast as she could to her car.

A sudden and frightening premonition sent cold chills up her spine as she climbed behind the wheel. Involving Georgio in her search might turn out to be the worst mistake of her life.

THE REST OF the day passed at a slow crawl. When she heard the cleaning crew outside her door, she glanced up at the clock. It was 7:00 p.m. No wonder the office had grown so quiet.

One of the maids stuck her head inside Faith's office. "You're so quiet I didn't realize you were still here."

"I'm wrapping up. I'll be out of your way in about ten minutes."

"Don't hurry for me. I got all night in this building. I can always come back and catch your office."

"I need to get of here, anyway." Not that she had anywhere to go but her empty house.

She used to love her job. Loved the challenges it presented and the office camaraderie. She hadn't loved anything for the past ten months, but the routine kept her occupied and the work kept her sane.

Thunder was rumbling in the distance by the time she reached home, and bolts of lightning created a fiery display as a storm rolled in. Huge drops began to splatter on her windshield as she pulled into the driveway.

She wondered if Cornell was watching the same storm blow in. When he was little he'd come running to her bed at the first clap of thunder. That had been so long ago.

She'd hoped to hear from Travis this afternoon with news of helpful information he'd gained from the analysis of Cornell's computer. He hadn't called. Neither had Georgio.

New pangs of guilt hit as she closed the garage door and then stepped into the mudroom. She hated lying to Travis about Georgio. Hated it so much she'd almost called him a couple times this afternoon. Once she'd actually started punching in his number before she broke the connection and put her phone away.

Even now she was tempted to call him. She could invite him over for dinner. Stupid idea. He was a busy cop. He'd call when he had news. He wouldn't be interested in spending the evening with a desperate mother who did nothing but whine and wallow in missing her almost-grown son.

If only she knew Cornell was safe.

Thunder hit again, this time so loud it rattled the windows. She made herself a sandwich, poured a glass of white wine and settled in front of the TV.

She was just in time to catch the hook for the evening news.

"Tonight at ten, Lieutenant Marilyn Sylvester of the Dallas Police Department will give further details about the murder of Scott Mitchell, the seventeen-year-old Dallas high-school student whose body was found floating in the Trinity River last week."

The bite of sandwich in Faith's mouth suddenly tasted like cardboard. This was the reason she'd practically quit watching TV altogether. News of murders or abductions gnawed at her stomach and her control like rabid rats. She turned off the set and picked up a magazine.

She thumbed through the pages. Beautiful women dressed in the latest fashion. Probably the kind of women Travis dated. Women who were fun and made him laugh, with no problems more significant than what color to paint their nails that week.

Or he might have a special woman in his life, maybe even a live-in. Only if he did, he hadn't brought her to the wedding. But that didn't mean he wasn't making out with her right now.

"Jeez!"

Faith tossed the magazine back to the coffee table. What was wrong with her that she was having these bizarre and unwanted thoughts about Travis? It had to be the apprehension. Or maybe just a crazy need to have a man to hold on to.

Only no other man affected her the way Travis did. Certainly Georgio hadn't.

Determined to push any sensual thoughts about Travis from her mind, she tossed the sandwich and went to do a load of laundry.

As she did she said a silent prayer that Cornell was safe and would call again tonight. And this time he'd tell her where to find him.

The phone rang two hours later, just as Faith was climbing into bed. Her heart jumped to her throat. She grabbed the phone with both hands and held it to her ear.

"Cornell."

"No."

The voice was soft and feminine. Her next words were icy, fearful, yet threatening.

Chapter Seven

"Stay away from Georgio."

Faith steadied the phone in her hand and kicked off the light blanket. Still reconciling herself to disappointment that the caller wasn't Cornell, she let the woman's words sink in.

"Who is this?" she demanded.

"Someone who knows what you're up to. I'm warning you, back off before you make things a hundred times worse."

"Worse for who? You? Georgio?"

"Yes. And for your son."

The words sent shock waves of dread rushing through Faith. She struggled to breathe. "If you know where my son is, please tell me. I beg you. Just tell me where he is."

"If he wanted you to know, he'd call you himself. Just back off and leave him be."

"I can help him. I will help him. He needs me."

But there was no one to hear the last of her words. The connection had gone dead.

Faith tried to call the number back. Not surprisingly, there was no answer. She was being jerked around. But by whom? Who would know she'd seen Georgio today?

The answer was obvious: anyone who happened to see

her in the Passion Pit today. Maybe even Travis, though he hadn't seen her. The only way he'd know she'd been there was if someone had told him.

It wouldn't have been Georgio. He'd made it clear he didn't want the cops to know he was involved in the search. But that left the hostess, perhaps a bartender or any number of employees that she hadn't noticed but who might have seen her.

And one of them did not want Faith anywhere near Georgio. Which meant the woman had to know what had happened to Cornell. She might even be behind his disappearance.

Faith needed to talk to Travis. He was a cop. He should be able to get a handle on the threat. Only discussing this with him would mean she'd have to level with him about seeing Georgio.

She rolled over and pounded her fists into her pillow, so hard that a few feathers started poking through the case. Why hadn't she given him at least a few days before defying all his stupid rules?

When her need to pummel something passed, she got up and went to the kitchen. God, she hated this empty house. It creaked and echoed, and tonight it even spit accusations at her.

Well, actually, it was rain pelting the windows and not spit she heard, but it had the same bewildering effect. She poured herself a glass of cold buttermilk, a habit she'd picked up from her granddad when she was just a kid.

He'd insisted that the clabbered cream had a soothing effect on his stomach and his mind when he couldn't sleep. It didn't work for her, but weirdly, she'd developed a taste for it. A curse of being Southern, her Yankee grandma had teased. Thanks to her mother's rebellious nature, Faith had spent far too little time with her grand-parents before they and their small car had been crushed by an eighteen-wheeler. They'd died two days before Faith's twelfth birthday. To this day, she missed them.

Faith took the milk and walked out to the covered deck, which took up about half the backyard. She dropped to a rocker and sat in the dark, watching and listening to the steady rainfall as it puddled on the lawn and rushed through the downspout.

Thoughts of her own parents filled her mind. She'd never really known her father. He and her mother had never married and he'd never been part of her life.

But there had been plenty of men around. Her mother had been involved with a series of boyfriends, marrying three of them.

She'd been going through her third divorce when Faith had met Melvin Ashburn, a surprise guest at her seventeenth birthday party. He'd introduced her to marijuana, alcohol and sex.

And pregnancy.

But she'd never expected to face that kind of rebellion with Cornell.

Faith set the empty glass on the deck beside her, leaned back and closed her eyes. Going over the past wouldn't help. She had to deal with the here and now. Things were no longer at a standstill.

The buttermilk was useless. She should have had a whiskey.

She got up, stretched and started to walk back inside. As she did, she had the creepy feeling that someone was watching her.

Add paranoia to the mix of anguished emotions attacking her soul.

"I KNOW THE MEDIA is clamoring for a juicy ratings booster, Chief, but we're not dealing with a serial killer out randomly targeting innocent teenage boys."

"We have four unsolved murders in eighteen months, Travis. All boys aged eighteen or under. No suspects."

"Three of those were known gang members and drug dealers. Get rid of drug smugglers like Georgio and you might stop some of those senseless murders."

"Then get the goods on Georgio."

"I'm getting closer," Travis assured him.

"But this last victim wasn't a drug dealer or a gang member," the chief said.

"We don't know that for certain yet."

"That's the problem. We don't know much. I need a suspect on this last murder before the mayor has my ass on the line."

"We're working on it."

"So, do you and Reno have any evidence, or is this just a guessing game?"

"I have a hunch." That was it, and not much of a hunch at that.

"Trying to tie this one to Georgio, too?"

"Not to the man himself," Travis admitted. "He'd never get his own hands bloody. But the victim had been seen in the Passion Pit a few times before he was killed."

The chief scratched his whiskered chin. "Damn. I thought sexting was supposed to be taking the place of strippers." He threw up his hands. "That remark was not for citizen consumption."

"Gotcha."

"Good. Now go out and find me a suspect before I get a Mothers March on the precinct. And before someone else's son comes up dead."

Travis knew the chief. The last statement was his real

concern. It was Travis' as well. That was why he had to find Cornell Ashburn fast. He had to make sure he wasn't their next victim.

He pushed up his sleeve and checked his watch. Almost five o'clock and still no word on Cornell's computer analysis. If Travis didn't hear something soon, he'd give Clark a call.

He went back to his office and back to work. He was still hard at it when one of the clerks came in and dropped a fax on his desk.

"This just came. I figured you might be waiting around for it."

"Thanks."

Travis started to read. Clark had come through for him again. The surprises started on page two of the printout. Either Faith Ashburn had been lying to him or she had no idea what her son had been into.

It was time to get down and dirty. The fairy tales were officially off the table.

FAITH SET THE round iron table on the deck with plates, silverware, napkins and two tall glasses of water. She considered adding wineglasses and a bottle of merlot, but had no doubt that even though Travis had suggested bringing Chinese, tonight's meeting was business.

There had been no missing his avoidance when she'd asked about the findings from Cornell's computer. She was almost sure she wouldn't like what he had to tell her.

Table set and with a few minutes to spare, she went back to her bedroom to freshen up. Instead, she stood in the doorway, staring at the phone and feeling fresh pangs of guilt. Would she ever make it through the night without blurting out the truth about Georgio and the latest phone call?

She forced her eyes from the phone and her feet to her dressing table. She never wore much makeup, but even that was long gone today. Her hair was slightly tousled, but she left it like that and brushed a smidgen of color onto her cheeks and lips.

Unzipping her black pencil skirt, a staple of her work wardrobe, she stepped out of it. White shorts, she decided. Casual but chic with the black-and-white pullover she was already wearing.

Not that her appearance mattered. This wasn't a date. She didn't even remember dating. Well, she did, but only because her last one had been a disaster. It had ended with her throwing up on the man's shoes.

She'd go easy on the Chinese tonight. As rattled as her nerves were, there was definitely the possibility of an encore performance.

The doorbell rang. She yanked up the zipper on her shorts and hurried to the entry. *Please just let there be good news about Cornell.*

"HOPE YOU'RE HUNGRY," Travis said when she opened the door. Both his arms were busy juggling cartons of food. A bottle of red wine was tucked precariously under his right elbow.

"Oops. I should have told you I've already eaten this year."

He grinned. "I may have gotten a little carried away while I was ordering, but it all looked so good. And I missed lunch. Maybe breakfast, too. It's hard to remember on an empty stomach."

She took a few of the cartons from him before he dropped them and sent noodles and sauce splattering across her floor. "Do you mind eating on the deck?"

"Would love it. I've been cooped up inside all day with

cops, criminals, the chief and other undesirables. What can I help you with?"

"You can open the wine. The corkscrew is in the top drawer next to the fridge."

"I can handle that. Not sure if the vino's decent, but the salesman at the liquor store said it goes well with Chinese. I'm usually a beer man myself, pop a top and drink it straight from a longneck."

"So what's the occasion?"

"I fake a little sophistication from time to time."

He was trying too hard to keep things light. That could only mean bad news. She made a couple trips outside with the food and wineglasses. When she opened the cartons, sweet and spicy odors escaped and her stomach began to roll.

Travis joined her as she dropped into a chair. He filled the wineglasses and then took the seat opposite hers. He held up his glass for a toast. "To a quick and successful search for Cornell."

A surge of hope swept through Faith as she clinked her glass with his. "Does this mean you found something helpful on his computer?"

"We definitely have new information to work with. It could be helpful." Travis passed her a container. "Shrimp fried rice. Hope you're not allergic to seafood."

"No." She put a spoonful on her plate and passed it back to him. He piled his plate high and took a bite before reaching for the next container.

He might be hungry, but he wasn't starving, not the way she was for news. "What new information?"

Travis forked up another bite of fried rice. "Why don't we eat and then get down to business?"

"I can't eat until I know."

He nodded while he chewed and finally swallowed. "What do you know about Angela Pointer?"

"I've never heard of her."

Travis wiped his mouth on his napkin and took a sip of wine. "Evidently, she and your son were an item."

"When?"

"Just before his disappearance. Are you sure he never mentioned her?"

"Not only did he never mention her, but neither did any of his friends when I questioned them. Was she a student in his high school?"

"He didn't know her from school. Angela's officially an exotic dancer, or at least she was when she and Cornell were exchanging hot and heavy emails."

"There must be some mistake. If Cornell had been serious about someone, he'd have told me about her. He's always told me about his crushes."

"This appeared to be more than a crush. The two of them were apparently spending a lot of time together."

"He was home most nights—except when he was studying with friends." And he had done that a lot just before his disappearance.

Even as Faith protested, her doubts were growing. Involvement with an exotic dancer would explain his being at the Passion Pit. She'd never been able to buy that he'd inappropriately touched a stripper. Being aggressive was against his very nature.

But if he and the young woman were sexually involved, their touching might have been seen as inappropriate by other employees or by Georgio.

Faith could even buy that he'd kept the relationship a secret from her, knowing she would have disapproved. But where was he now? Where was Angela?

More confused and disturbed than ever, Faith opened

her wooden chopsticks and used them to push her food around on the plate. When she looked up, she realized that Travis had stopped eating and was watching her.

She met his penetrating gaze and knew the worst might be yet to come. "There's more, isn't there?"

"A little."

"You may as well hit me with all of it," she said.

"Angela was pregnant."

"Pregnant?" Faith's spirits took another plunge. This girlfriend she'd never even heard of had been pregnant ten months ago. The baby would have been born by now. An ache swelled inside her, but still her mind refused to wrap itself around the obvious implications.

"That doesn't mean Cornell was the father," she insisted. "I can't believe he would have kept my own grandchild a secret from me—not for months."

I'm sorry. I'm so sorry...

Cornell's words echoed in her head, haunting, tearing at her soul. Was this what he was sorry for? Getting a woman pregnant and running away with her? Putting Faith through hell for the past ten months?

But why? Why wouldn't he come to her? And where would he have gone with no money? The woman could hardly have worked at that profession while she was pregnant.

She looked away, hating for Travis to see the tears burning in her eyes. She didn't see him reach across the table, but felt his hands close around hers.

Big hands. Rough skin, yet the touch was gentle. Comforting. Protective.

"I'm sorry I had to tell you like this, but I couldn't think of an easy way to break it to you."

"It's not your fault. I asked for the truth. It's just hard to swallow."

"Look on the bright side," Travis said. "This makes it a lot more likely your son left of his own free will and that there was no foul play involved."

Travis was right, of course, yet her heart felt incredibly heavy. For Cornell to have done something so irresponsible, for him to have disregarded her fears and feelings this way, would mean she didn't know her son at all.

Travis's thumbs stroked the back of her hands, but she wasn't sure he was even aware of the soothing motions. His brow was furrowed, his lips stretched into a tight line. She could envision theories whirring in his mind, none of them giving her the answers she craved.

Finally, she pulled her hands away and wrapped one around the stem of her wineglass. She tipped it up, stared into the swirling liquid and then took a large sip. She couldn't avoid reality just because it didn't suit her.

"Looks like I wasn't the mother I thought I was."

"Don't go judging yourself. Teenagers are famous for making bad decisions. Besides, I have an idea we've just scratched the surface in this investigation."

"It was a deep scratch."

"It opened lots of possibilities, but we can't be certain that Cornell was the baby's father or that the girlfriend was even pregnant. It could have been a trap to get money out of him."

"He had no money."

"She might not have known that."

"That doesn't explain his dropping off the face of the earth for ten months."

"Until the phone call the other night," Travis reminded her—as if she could forget. "He's made the first step toward reaching out to you, and even though it sent you into panic mode, I have to think it's a good sign."

She couldn't argue the point in light of all she'd learned tonight. It didn't lessen her desperation to find him.

"We have to locate this Angela person," Faith said. "Have you checked to see if she's still working at the Passion Pit or if anyone there knows how to get in touch with her?"

"Not yet. I wanted to talk to you first."

Faith considered her options. She could talk to Georgio herself now that he'd agreed to help find Cornell. There was no reason to think he wouldn't level with her.

Pangs of guilt attacked again. She felt as if she was two-timing Travis, creating a lovers' triangle. How crazy was that?

Nonetheless, she had to tell Travis she'd talked to Georgio. If not tonight, then soon. She'd never been able to stomach lies and deceit, and this was proving to be no exception.

She forced down a few bites of food while Travis ate ravenously. He ate like a man with an appetite and appreciation for the tastes and smells and textures. She'd be willing to bet he jumped into life with that same gusto.

No holds barred. No limits. Daring the odds to play against him.

"Have you ever been afraid of anything or anyone, Travis?"

He stopped eating and looked up, his dark eyes meeting hers. "Sure. Probably wouldn't be alive today if I didn't have a healthy fear of thugs and addicts with guns."

"That's wisdom and caution. I'm talking about real fear."

He put down his fork and wiped his mouth with the napkin. "I was scared to death when I was little, sure the monster that my foster mother told me would get me was waiting for dark to come, and me to close my eyes, before it snapped me up and ate me."

Faith shuddered. "Your foster mother frightened you like that?"

"One of them did. She was a real sweetheart."

"I'm sorry."

"Don't be. I got over it. What doesn't kill you makes you stronger and a hell of a lot smarter."

"So monsters, that's it?"

"There was this two-ton bull a few years back. Wanted to show me who was boss after he threw me off his back and into the dirt. When I saw that hoof coming at my head, I knew a moment or two of panic."

"Ouch." She cringed at the image. "You could have been killed."

"Yep. That's the night I gave up bull riding for keeps. Figured I could do more good as a cop than a corpse, so here I am."

Here he was, on her deck, chatting as easily as if they'd known each other for years. A knight in cowboy boots and carrying a badge. He'd found out more about her son in two days than the DPD missing-persons division, the P.I. she'd hired and she with all her questions had discovered in ten long months.

"So the Western boots you wear are not just for show. You really are a cowboy."

"Every chance I get." He scooted back from the table, stretching his long legs in front of him. "I know I hit you with a lot tonight, Faith. I know how worried you are about Cornell. But give me a little more time. I promise I'll find him. If he's in any kind of trouble, I'll go in and even the odds. Trust me on that."

Strangely, she did. She owed him big-time. But she couldn't deny that it was more than gratitude he inspired.

She liked his being here, liked his touch when he'd held her hands across the small table. Even liked watching him eat.

If she wasn't very careful, she might start liking him so much that she forgot he was here only as a cop and as a favor to his brother's bride.

When they finished eating, Travis gathered the nearly empty food containers and carried them to the trash while Faith cleared the dishes from the table. "Leave the wine and glasses," he suggested. "I have a few more questions and it's too nice outdoors to go inside yet."

"Questions about Cornell?"

"Yeah, though feel free to wow me with your personal exploits if you like. You've heard my tales of horror and stupid acts of daring."

"You were in attendance during my most stupid act of daring," she said.

"Fighting off the drunk at the Passion Pit?"

"In full hooker garb."

"Do you still have that outfit?" He grinned devilishly.

"No," she lied.

"Yet it lives forever in my mind."

She made a face. "Now, that's scary."

But not nearly as scary as the zany pulses of sensuality she felt at his teasing. "I'll finish in here," she said, before the sudden flushes of heat inside her grew any hotter. "I'll meet you back on the patio in a few minutes."

"Sounds good."

"But no more wine for me," she said. "I'm a light-weight drinker." And not used to sexual temptation in any shape or form, certainly not the shape and form of a rugged cowboy cop on a night when, thanks to Cornell's secrets, her vulnerability was at an all-time high.

TRAVIS RETURNED TO the deck, worrying that the questions he needed to ask were only going to upset Faith more. But Cornell was clearly not the innocent schoolboy Faith had portrayed him as. He was a man, albeit young and probably inexperienced.

Messing around with one of Georgio's dancers could have led him into real trouble. Travis only hoped that actually had been Cornell and not an imposter who'd made that phone call in the wee hours of the morning. His being alive was the best news they could have hoped for.

It was Cornell's connection to Georgio through Angela Pointer that worried Travis the most. Georgio ruled his world like a third-world dictator. No one crossed him. No one ratted on him. He made sure they were too scared to do that.

Travis poured himself a half glass of wine and walked to the edge of the deck, his thoughts wandering back to Faith. Her heart was literally breaking with worry over Cornell.

His mother must have felt that same kind of love for him and Leif. She'd left R.J., her sorry, alcoholic, womanizing husband, and raised them by herself.

Only instead of losing him or Leif, she'd lost her own battle with cancer, knowing she was leaving two young sons to make it without her.

Travis wished he remembered more, but most of what he knew of her came from Leif. She had loved them more than anything. Leif had assured him of that. Travis figured that if she were alive today, she'd like Faith.

He liked her, too. More than *liked*. He didn't understand it himself, but some weird chemistry had come into play the first night he met her. She'd stayed on his mind, haunted his dreams, fueled more than a few fantasies.

But then she'd been more image than person. Now

she was real. She was a key component of an investigation that might link to a lot more than Cornell's running off with a stripper.

No two ways about it. Faith ignited urges and feelings in him that had no place in a police investigation. Reactions like those made lawmen weak and all too frequently stupid. The brain tended to check out when emotions checked in.

He looked up as Faith rejoined him on the porch. The sun had set and the moonlight filtering through the branches of a stately oak tree painted silver streaks in her silky brown hair.

The crazy need to take her in his arms and hold her close hit again. Damn. Why did this have to be so hard? She was attractive, but she was just a woman. He worked with them all the time. None had ever gotten to him like this.

"What else do you want to know?" she asked.

"Anything that might help me to get inside Cornell's head, figure out what and how he'd react to stressful situations."

"After what you told me tonight, I'm not sure how well I even knew him."

"Let's start with the seizures," Travis said, needing her to focus on specifics. "Was this something new or had he dealt with them for a long time?"

"They started when he was fourteen. Cornell's father was working for a Central American oil company at the time. Cornell went for a two-week visit. A few days after he came home, he started running a high fever. The seizures started soon after."

And that had surely scared her to death. "How long was he sick?"

"Two weeks. He was finally diagnosed with some rare

strain of flu. Twice we were told he might not make it through the night."

Faith's voice broke. She swayed and then leaned against a corner post for support. Travis could fight it no longer. He walked over and put an arm around her shoulders.

She leaned into him, her head nestled against his chest. His thumb rode the tight veins in her neck.

"I'm sorry," she finally whispered between sniffles. "I've relived this often enough that I should be able to talk about it without falling to pieces. It's just that everything is so stressful right now."

"No apology needed." He'd always figured he'd had a tough life growing up, but Faith's hadn't been a picnic. A divorce. Raising a son alone. And now this. "You've earned the right to a little meltdown," he said.

"But it doesn't change anything."

She stepped from his arms. They felt incredibly empty without her.

Travis's cell phone vibrated. He was tempted to ignore it, but was too much a cop to do that. He checked the caller ID. It was his partner, Reno.

He took the call. "What's up?"

"You know that dancer you asked me to run through the system?"

"Yeah."

"No rap sheet, but she's a runaway. Lived with her mother and stepfather in West Texas before she left home at sixteen."

"And since then?"

"Worked at a convenience store in Austin before ending up in Dallas and going to work as an exotic dancer at the Passion Pit. But get this, she made a 911 call a couple of weeks before Cornell disappeared. Said her boyfriend had beat her up and she needed an ambulance.

Spent two days in the hospital, then dropped charges against the guy."

"Do you have an ID on him?"

"Walt Marshall. Also one of Georgio's employees."

"Subject ever been married?"

"I take it you're not free to talk right now?"

"Not really, but go on. Where is Marshall now?"

"Missing in action, at least from the Dallas area. Never reported as missing, but I can't find anything on him for the last ten months."

"Anything else on the subject?"

"According to her landlady, Angela Pointer left about the same time Cornell disappeared, without paying her rent. That's all I've got so far. So you want to tell me what this is all about?"

"Yeah. I'll call you back in about ten minutes."

He wasn't going to get into this with Faith until he had more facts. But it was turning into one hell of a mess.

Travis didn't even want to speculate what kind of trouble Cornell had gotten himself into if he was messing around with the pregnant girlfriend of a lunatic.

"An emergency?" Faith asked when he broke the connection.

"Appears that way. I hate to rush off, but my partner has some new evidence on one of our cases and I need to go over it with him."

"No problem. I understand completely. I can't thank you enough for what you've already done."

"I'll check out Angela Pointer tomorrow," he promised. In truth, he planned to do a little snooping tonight. "I'll get back to you as soon as I find out anything further. In the meantime, call me if you hear from Cornell again."

"I will."

She walked him back through the house and to the

front door. When she looked up at him, he got hit with that crazy rush of emotions again. He had to make the goodbye short and not too sweet before he did something really foolish—like kiss her.

"Lock your door," he cautioned. "You can't be too careful in the big city."

"I always do."

He took one of her hands, squeezed it tightly and then turned and walked away while he still could.

With any luck he'd find Angela Pointer alive and well and swinging from a pole at the Passion Pit tonight. He had an ugly hunch that wouldn't be the case.

Chapter Eight

"They were lying," Reno said as they walked back to Travis's pickup truck.

"The two dancers who actually admitted knowing Angela?"

"Yeah. Their spiel sounded rehearsed."

"Right," Travis agreed. "I don't figure I'll do any better talking to Georgio when he gets back in town—if he's actually out of town."

Reno opened the door and swung into the passenger side. "Easy to see how Ethridge hit a brick wall."

"We've already gotten a few steps further than he did," Travis said as he slid behind the wheel. "At least we know about Angela Pointer."

"But not her whereabouts," his partner said emphatically. "Nor are you any closer to locating Cornell. And lest you forget, we are in the middle of a very high-profile murder investigation."

"All true. But I promised Faith Ashburn I'd find her son, and I never walk on a promise. Besides, I'm not totally convinced Scott's murder and Cornell's disappearance are exclusive."

"Now you're pushing it. Eighteen-year-old runs off with his sexy girlfriend—not the kind you take home to Mama—then calls his mother months later and says

'I'm sorry.' Doesn't sound like foul play to me," Reno said. "Sounds like a teenager whose hormones are calling all the shots."

"Normally, I'd agree with you, but Faith is so sure he wouldn't have left home."

"The same Faith who didn't even know her son was boinking a stripper?"

"I know. It doesn't all add up, but having Georgio involved in this in any way makes me naturally suspicious. Add the abusive boyfriend to that mix and there's plenty of reason to worry."

"I still don't see a connection with Scott Mitchell."

"I know. Just call it one of my wild hunches." Travis started the engine, shifted into gear and pulled into traffic. It was light even for a Tuesday night.

"So tell me again. Exactly how are you connected to Cornell's mother?"

"She's a good friend of Leif's new wife, maid of honor at the wedding."

"So no kin to you?"

"None."

"Good-looking?" Reno asked.

Easy to see where this was going. "What does that have to do with anything?"

"Just curious."

"She's attractive."

"And unattached."

"It appears that way, but I'm not doing this just so I can jump her bones, if that's what you're insinuating."

"Actually, that would make a lot more sense than any other reason you've given for jumping headfirst into Ethridge's case. About damn time you jumped somebody's bones. Might make you a lot less irritable."

"Well, it won't be Faith Ashburn's, not until her son is found, and probably not then."

"Why not? Too old for you?"

"Nope."

"Too hot for you?"

"Too complicated." And too damned irresistible. The kind who'd make you think of forever. Travis was not a forever guy.

"Complicated? What the hell is that supposed to mean? She smarter than you are?"

"Probably. Most women I date are. But the complicated part is if we date and she gets serious."

"Break up like you always do when a girlfriend gets serious."

"Only with Faith, that wouldn't be the end of it. I'd have my brother's wife mad at me. Would make those family gatherings real chummy. Plus I'd have to worry about running into her if I showed up at the Dry Gulch to visit Leif."

"That's all a bunch of B.S. Face it, partner. You're falling for her and it's scaring you to death."

"Not a chance. Cops and marriage are a lousy mix. You're the only one in Homicide not divorced or cheating on your wife."

Reno laughed and gave him a friendly punch to the arm. "Yep, already thinking about marriage. You're all but roped and tied. Can't wait until I meet Faith. She must be a hell of a woman."

"She is. But this is about finding her son, and that's the only place our relationship is going."

But in spite of his denial, Travis was having a devil of a time keeping Faith off his mind.

He wondered what Leif would say about that. But then Leif was probably the wrong one to ask. He'd fallen madly in love with Joni in a matter of days. And now he was living at the Dry Gulch Ranch with a father he'd always claimed to hate.

Must be something in the water. Travis would stick to beer.

FAITH LOOKED UP from the notes she was going over, and punched the buzzer to retrieve the message from her secretary. "You have a caller on line one, a man, says it's personal."

"Did he give a name?"

"No, but he said this was about Cornell."

Her heart lurched. "Thanks. I'll take the call."

"Good morning, Faith. Hope I didn't catch you at a bad time."

"Georgio." She hadn't expected to hear from him this soon—or at this number. "The timing is fine. I'm busy, but I always am. I just didn't remember mentioning to you where I work."

"You didn't, but information like that is easy to find. I tried your cell-phone number first. There was no answer."

"I just got out of a meeting and I'd turned it off." She pulled the cell from her desk drawer and checked it as she talked. Sure enough, one missed call.

Cautious anticipation surged. "This must be important for you to call me at work."

"Something I find worrisome, but I'd rather not talk about it on the phone. I was hoping you could meet me for lunch."

She checked her watch. Eleven-thirty, and she had a meeting at one. But anxiety had replaced anticipation now and she wouldn't be able to concentrate on anything until she heard what Georgio had to say.

"I can get away for a little while, but I need to be back here a few minutes before one."

"Perfect. I'm on my way to the airport, but I built in a little time in case you were available. I can pick you up in front of your office in about ten minutes."

"I'll be there." Hopefully, Georgio's worrisome news was the same information she'd already gotten from Travis and not something else to complicate matters. No use speculating. She'd know in a matter of minutes.

As far as she was concerned, they could bypass lunch and talk in the car. In fact, she'd suggest it. That way she wouldn't have to wait to hear what he had to say, and he could go straight to the airport.

She filed the reports from the morning, took a quick bathroom break and then rode the elevator down to the first floor. She walked out the double glass doors right on time.

A black luxury car was stopped in front of the building. A chauffeur stepped out and opened the back door for her. Georgio leaned over and waved a welcome.

So much for talking in the car. She climbed into the backseat, straightening and tugging her skirt down to cover most of her thighs when she noticed Georgio ogling them. As if he didn't see enough flesh in his nightclubs.

"There's a small bistro around the corner," he said. "The menu is limited, but Chef François is creative and the food exquisite. I took the liberty of making reservations there. I trust that's agreeable."

"Anyplace is fine with me as long as we can talk."

"We'll have a private room."

Her apprehension burgeoned. Was what he had to tell her so alarming that he couldn't chance it being overheard? Or was he afraid of her reaction when she heard what he had to say?

The short ride to the bistro seemed endless.

Once they were inside, the maître d's welcome was officious as he showed them to a private room and a white-linen-covered table. A bottle of wine was open, two crystal stems already filled with the rich purple liquid.

"I never drink when I'm working," she said.

"Not a problem," Georgio assured her as he held out her chair. "It's just that our time is so limited, I ordered ahead. François has prepared a few special treats."

"I'm sure they will be delicious, but right now food is the least of my concerns," she said, cutting short his irrelevant verbiage. "I'm too nervous to wait any longer to hear what you learned about Cornell."

"Yes, of course," he said. "I hate to upset you, but I think you should be aware of what's going on."

"Which is?"

"Two of my dancers at the Passion Pit called me this morning, both of them very upset over being informally questioned by two homicide detectives last night."

The tightness in Faith's chest relaxed a bit. One of the detectives was no doubt Travis, following up on what he'd learned about Angela Pointer.

"Exactly what about the visit upset them?"

"From the questions they were asked, they think Angela Pointer, one of my former employees, may have been murdered."

"Did the detectives say that?"

"Not directly."

"Then why would they assume she's been murdered?"

"All I know is that both of my employees got that same impression."

Dread vibrated through Faith. Travis had definitely not insinuated that with her. "Was there any mention of Cornell?"

Georgio looked down before making eye contact. Concern was etched into every line of his face.

"I'm afraid so. I hate telling you this, Faith. And remember, we're just going on the assumptions made by two ladies who were questioned. But it sounds to me as if the police are looking to pin Angela's murder on your son."

Fear and anger collided inside Faith with such sickening force she was afraid she might pass out. Georgio was wrong. He had to be wrong. Travis was trying to find Cornell, not convict him.

François interrupted the damning conversation to greet Georgio and personally serve an appetizer of champagne-truffle mousse pâté and a promise of more culinary delights to follow.

Faith struggled to pull herself together. She had to stay focused, had to concentrate on the facts.

"What was said to make them reach such a bizarre conclusion?"

"It was pretty clear from the leading questions the detectives asked, and I'm afraid the answers the ladies gave them didn't help Cornell's case."

"What did they say?"

"The truth, so you can't blame them."

"What truth?"

"That Angela was being stalked by someone she described as being just a kid with overactive hormones. She said he'd followed her home on several occasions and had somehow gotten her email address. He was sending her notes saying he loved her and that they were meant to be together, that sort of thing."

"That doesn't sound like Cornell," Faith said. And it was definitely not the way Travis had described the email communication. "Did Angela mention Cornell's name to them?"

"If she did, they didn't remember."

"If that's the case, why didn't they go to the police with that information when Angela went missing?"

"Because Angela called me and told me there was a family emergency and she was moving back to West Texas. I told the others, and none of us suspected anything different."

"Cornell would never stalk anyone, much less harm them. I know that. I know my son." Faith would not use the word *murder,* could not let herself think it.

This couldn't be happening. Travis had come to her at the reception and offered to help find Cornell. He'd told her she could trust him. Had it all been a ruse to get her to help him find her son, only to put him behind bars?

She'd played right into his hands. Given him Cornell's computer for a forensic analysis. For all she knew, he'd even lied to her about what he'd found on it.

She pushed back from the table. "Is there anything else I should know?"

"Only that I want to help you find your son and clear his name."

"Why? You don't know him. You don't know me."

"But what I do know of you, I like. You're a sensitive woman concerned about your son. I respect that. And I don't trust the cops. Never have. That's why I insisted you not tell them that you've talked to me. Believe me, they'll discredit me and all my intentions. And they'll make my work in locating Cornell even more difficult. You can trust me."

Trust. She wasn't sure she'd trust anyone ever again. Not if Cornell was a suspect in a young woman's murder.

Could it be possible that he knew that? Was that the reason he was afraid to come home?

Alone. Afraid. And innocent. Cornell would never hurt anyone. Never. She'd stake her life on that.

The waiter walked in and set a bowl of lobster bisque in front of each of them.

Faith pushed hers away and stood. She couldn't sit here another minute without going mad. She grabbed her handbag from the back of her chair. "I have to go."

"You should try to eat something."

"I can't eat. Really, I have to go. I need to be alone to think."

"Whatever you say. I'll call for my driver."

"No. I don't want a driver. I'll walk back. It's not far and I need the fresh air."

"If you insist. I'll call you when I get back to town in a few days, but in the meantime, don't talk to the cops, and if you hear from Cornell, phone me at once."

All she could manage was a nod. She bumped into the maître d' as she rushed from the private room, mumbled an apology and kept going.

Barely aware of the traffic or the warmth from the sun seeping through her blouse, she almost ran the few blocks back to her office. Once there, she stared at the doors, but couldn't make herself go inside. She kept walking, not stopping until she reached a nearby coffee shop.

She ordered an espresso, took it to a back table and put the cup to her lips and sipped. The burn of heat and bitterness washed into her empty stomach.

She'd finished the coffee before her mind cleared enough that she knew what she had to do. Still, her hands shook as she punched Travis's cell number into her phone.

She would not be used as a pawn by Detective Travis Dalton. She'd demand he tell her the truth.

And to think she'd been worried she was falling hard for the traitorous cowboy cop.

DAZED TO THE POINT she could barely function, Faith managed to stumble through the one-o'clock meeting before she gave up and took the rest of the day off. She'd thought she'd been through a lot, with concerns for Cornell's health and then the terror of his sudden disappearance.

Nothing had prepared her for this. Cornell, a suspect in a murder case. On top of it all, she felt betrayed. A fool for taking a homicide detective at his word.

Please come home, Cornell. We can get through this together the way we always have.

Why hadn't she said that in the few seconds he'd been on the phone?

Faith closed the garage door and stepped into her mudroom. She hesitated by the back door as a disturbing sensation swept through her.

Something was different than when she'd left this morning. Nothing obvious, just a feeling. No. A faint but unfamiliar odor. She looked around. Everything was in place. Nothing appeared to be touched.

She definitely had to add paranoia to her growing list of problems.

Still, she scanned the area cautiously as she walked back to her bedroom and kicked off her shoes. She checked her landline phone for messages. There were none, meaning not only that Travis hadn't called back on that number, but that her prayers for a call from Cornell had not been answered.

She changed into a pair of cropped jeans and a bright pink T-shirt, then walked barefoot to the kitchen for a glass of cold water. She stopped in her tracks when the soles of her feet felt something gritty.

Her shattered nerves reacted with a new wave of apprehension. She was certain she hadn't spilled anything this morning.

Impulsively, she walked over and pulled a sharp chef's knife from the wooden block on the countertop. Not that she'd ever used a knife as a weapon before. Not that she'd ever used a weapon, for that matter.

She dropped to her knees for a closer look. The few grains of gritty substance were easier to feel than to see. She'd probably tracked in whatever it was herself when she'd stepped outside for the morning newspaper.

Her cell phone rang, jolting her back to reality from paranoiaville. She grabbed the phone from her pocket and checked the caller ID. Joni. Never had she needed to hear the voice of an old friend more. An old friend who didn't need to be saddled with Faith's problems on her honeymoon.

Faith took a deep breath and faked a normalcy to her tone. "Hello, honeymooner. Don't you have better things to do than call me?"

"Have to come up for air occasionally. What are you doing home this time of day?"

"What makes you think I'm home? You called me on my cell phone."

"I know, but I called your office first. Melanie said you'd left work early. That's not like you."

Faith swallowed hard. "I had a headache." Even a white lie didn't come easy, especially to Joni.

"Leif just got off the phone with Travis," her friend said.

The statement sounded like an indictment. Joni clearly knew more than Faith had anticipated. "Good. Nice that brothers keep in touch."

"Travis is worried about you, Faith."

So worried he hadn't bothered to call her back. "Did he call Leif just to tell him that?"

"No. Leif called him. He thinks Travis should visit the Dry Gulch Ranch and at least have a conversation with R.J. while he's still lucid."

"How did I get into that conversation?"

"Travis just said you were dealing with a lot right now and he thought it might be a good idea if I called you."

"He told you about Angela Pointer, didn't he?"

"A little," Joni admitted. "I know it was hard to face that Cornell had a life he kept secret from you, but I'm sure there are lots of teenage guys who don't tell their mothers everything."

"I know, but Cornell... I mean, we were so close. He was a good kid, always."

"I know. Travis is going to find him and get to the bottom of things. When he does, you and Cornell will be close again. Whatever went wrong, you can work through it."

Travis, the hero. Faith could take it no longer. "Travis's interest in Cornell goes a lot deeper than just bringing him home safely."

"What are you talking about?"

The accusations against the callous detective spilled straight from Faith's heart. Once she started, she couldn't stop. She left nothing out, from the computer analysis to her talk with Georgio.

By the time Faith stopped for breath, her voice was as shaky as her insides.

"Are you telling me that you'd believe what that flesh-and drug-peddling rat Georgio had to tell you over what Travis says?"

"It's not that I trust Georgio," Faith admitted. "But how would he know that Travis was even at the Passion

Pit last night unless he'd talked to the dancers who were questioned? His information came from them. Angela was their friend. They'd have no reason to lie."

"None that you know of. I don't know who knows what, Faith. Neither do you at this point. But I know my husband, and he knows his brother. If he says you can trust Travis to help you find Cornell, you can."

"And I know my son," Faith argued. "He didn't kill anyone. He couldn't."

"Then you don't have anything to worry about on that score. Tell Travis exactly what you told me, including Georgio's part in all of this. Travis will have a reasonable explanation. Give him a chance."

"Travis doesn't even want me talking to Georgio."

"Because he's a dangerous snake in the grass. Already he's poisoning your mind. You can't play Travis and Georgio against each other. Think this through, Faith. Trust Travis completely. He wants to help and he can help, the same way Leif saved my life."

She wanted to. More than anything, Faith wanted to trust Travis, but she would not throw her son to the lions. "I don't think I can do that, Joni."

"Then I'm coming home tonight to talk some sense into you."

"Don't you dare. A honeymoon is a onetime thing."

"Not for Leif and me. Our love grows deeper by the day."

The doorbell rang. "Someone's at the door," Faith said. "I need to go, but promise me you won't come rushing back to Texas."

"Then give Travis a chance to explain everything. Trust him."

"I'll listen to what he has to say." That was all she could promise.

She broke the connection as she padded though the house to the door.

She peeked through the peephole.

Travis stood there, a few feet away so that she saw his full six-feet-plus, imposing frame. A six-pack of beer dangled from his right hand as if he was expecting this to be a social call. The dark lock of hair that fell over his forehead made him look almost boyish.

But the jeans, the cowboy boots, a light blue shirt opened at the neck and an unbuttoned rust-colored sport coat swinging from his shoulder left no doubt that he was all man.

Her stomach fluttered, but this time she wouldn't be influenced by the traitorous sizzle of awareness he ignited in spite of everything she'd heard.

She swung open the door. "Come in, Travis."

"Sorry I missed your call. I was in a meeting with the chief of police and the mayor."

"I realize you're a very dedicated *homicide* detective."

"Busy, anyway. I tried to reach you at the office, but they said you'd left, so I took a chance on finding you here."

"Fine. We need to talk."

And this time she'd be asking the questions.

Chapter Nine

Travis had no idea what had set Faith off, but she was definitely in dragon-lady mode. Hopefully, it was something to do with work and not with Cornell.

He held up the six-pack. "Join me in a beer?"

"No, thank you, but you go ahead."

"Mind if I put the rest in your fridge?"

"Help yourself. I'll be on the deck."

He joined her a few minutes later, cold beer in hand. She was sitting in one of the outdoor chairs, legs crossed, her right one kicking like crazy. Her toenails were painted hot-pink. The cropped jeans showed off her terrific calves.

Travis took a sip of beer and then leaned his backside against the deck railing next to a pot of blooming pansies.

She stopped swinging her leg and shot him an accusing stare. "When did you decide to go after Cornell as a murder suspect?"

The bitter accusation caught him off guard. He set the beer down on the railing. "What the devil are you talking about?"

"No pretense, Travis. Just answer the question. Was it before Joni's wedding? Was that why you pretended to be so interested in helping me?"

He picked up his beer and drained at least a third of

the bottle while he tried to figure out was this sudden outbreak was all about. "I didn't pretend anything that night. It's not like I forced you to dance with me." Though he had coaxed.

"Then why trick me into turning over Cornell's computer so you could search for evidence to connect him to Angela Pointer?"

"Trick you?" He finished the beer and stepped in closer. "You wanted your son found. You were eager for me to see what was on his computer. And for the record, Angela was never even reported as missing and there's no indication she's dead. I don't know how you came up with the wild idea I was investigating her murder."

Faith's mouth drew so tight her luscious lips practically disappeared. "It makes sense. You're an overworked homicide detective, yet you take on a missing-person case the Dallas P.D. already said didn't indicate foul play. Why would you take on a missing-person case?"

Damn good question.

He let the truth rumble around in his head. Because he hadn't been able to get her off his mind after seeing her the very first time in the Passion Pit.

Because she'd turned him on like a brick oven when they danced to a belly-rubbing ballad at Leif's wedding.

All of which he was seriously starting to regret. He struggled for an answer that stayed close to the truth.

"You seemed convinced that your son didn't leave of his own accord, Faith. I'm a good judge of character. I believed you, which is more than you're giving me credit for right now. So let's get a few things straight."

"I just want the truth."

"And you're going to get it. I'm a cop, a damn good one. I don't pin murders on people. I discover evidence, not manufacture it, and I don't like comments that suggest otherwise.

"I didn't even know that Angela Pointer existed until I read the computer analysis. No one had ever reported her as missing, so there was no investigation into her whereabouts. If I find out she was murdered here in Dallas, you can bet that I or one of the other homicide detectives will do everything we can to find out who killed her.

"But you're right on one count. I have plenty to keep me busy and I don't push my help on women who don't want it. If you don't trust me, we need to break ties right now."

She stared at him without saying a word, which was pretty much answer enough.

"I'm going to the kitchen for another beer," he said. "You decide if you want me to hang around long enough to finish it."

Travis cursed himself under his breath as he walked to the kitchen. He hadn't reacted like a cop. He'd reacted like a man. Police investigations and lust were a mix guaranteed to create chaos. Every cop knew that. The smart ones stayed clear of it.

Normally, Travis was one of them.

He opened the fridge, took out one beer and then reached back in for another. A time-out might help both of them get the burrs out of their saddle blankets.

As angry as she'd made him, he didn't want to just walk away and leave things like this. Even if she kicked him out, he couldn't stop looking for Cornell.

He wasn't sure where Angela Pointer fit into the scheme of things, but whatever had sent Cornell on the run was most likely connected to Georgio Trosclair.

And if Travis's theory about Georgio was right, he ordered a person's murder as easily as most people ordered a pizza. Travis had spent the past year trying to prove that. He wouldn't stop until he did.

FAITH WALKED TO the railing and watched a bluebird swoop from the branches of a redbud tree to the tiny box where its babies waited to be fed. A protective, nurturing mom. Doing what came naturally, acting on instinct.

Faith wondered if she was doing the same. Acting on instinct where Cornell was concerned, jumping to conclusions, attacking Travis without even hearing his side of the story. But she couldn't just blindly trust him or let her attraction for him affect her in any way. Nor could she afford to turn away from him if he was actually trying to help her find Cornell.

Travis stepped out the back door, an open bottle of beer in each hand. He held one out to her. "I thought you might need this," he said.

She never drank beer. Bad for the waistline. This time she took it. She sipped it slowly and then walked over and sat down on the wide, wooden steps that led down to the lawn and her neatly planted butterfly garden. The blue phlox were already in bloom.

Travis dropped to the step beside her, not too close, but near enough she caught the light, woodsy fragrance of his aftershave. He leaned against the railing post, his long legs stretched in front of him, as he watched a honeybee flying among the blossoms sampling the nectar.

Faith studied his profile and then looked away quickly when she felt her resolve not to be affected by his heady masculinity begin to dissolve.

"Sorry for the explosion," she said, determined to keep everything in perspective. "I had a rough day."

"So I gathered. Is that why you left early?"

She nodded.

He didn't push for more. She drank a few more sips of beer, rehearsing in her mind what she had to say. Finally, she took a deep breath and dived in.

"The information about Angela Pointer preyed on my mind all day and I guess I let my imagination get out of hand."

His expression indicated he wasn't buying it, and the lies were starting to ferment and turn to acid in the pit of her stomach.

"I was so upset I became paranoid," she added.

He turned to face her. "And decided I couldn't be trusted. You sure jumped to that conclusion fast."

"Worse. I was paranoid about everything. When I came home from the office I thought someone had been in my house while I was away. I even picked up a knife to fight off the intruder who didn't exist."

"Does that happen often?"

"Never."

He leaned in closer. "What made you think there had been an intruder? Was something out of place?"

She shrugged, hating to admit what a wreck she'd become. "No. I detected an unfamiliar piney scent that reminded me of a man's aftershave, probably the smells of spring that came in with me when I'd opened the door."

Travis's expression darkened. "Anything else?"

"I was barefoot when I went into the kitchen and I stepped on what felt like spilled salt on the floor under the ceiling light fixture. When I looked closer, it was more like a chalky sand, no doubt something I tracked in myself."

"Makes sense. I wouldn't worry."

The grimace on his face didn't match his tone. He stood and studied the roof of the deck as intensely as if he were looking for killer spiders.

He put his finger to his lips to shush her even though she wasn't talking, and shot her a warning look she didn't understand. "I gotta be going," he said. "We can talk later if you want, but if you don't trust me, you should find someone else to look for your son."

Still holding his finger to his lips, he took her hand, tugged her to a standing position, and led her off the deck and onto the cushiony carpet of grass. He didn't speak until they reached the back gate of the fenced yard.

"Do you have a stepladder handy?" he said, his voice barely more than a whisper.

"What's going on, Travis?"

"Probably nothing, but I want to make sure that's the case."

"Do you think there actually might have been an intruder?"

"Yes, but I'm a cop. We tend to suspect the worst."

"Why the stepladder?"

"Playing a hunch, but just a hunch, so don't get upset yet. Just tell where to find the ladder."

"It's in the garage. I'll get it for you."

"No, I want you to stay in the yard until I get back. Don't even walk back to the deck."

If this was some trick to scare her into doing everything he said, it wasn't going to work. Yet her heart was pounding as she watched him walk away.

She grew more nervous by the second. By the time he returned twenty minutes later, her emotions were vacillating between fear and doubt. Without saying a word, he opened his hand so that she could see what he was holding. It was no bigger than a penlight battery.

"What is that?"

"A microphone. Turns out you're not paranoid. Your house has been bugged."

"Bugged. Who would do such a thing? What would they expect to learn from me?"

"I'm not sure, but I intend to find out. In the meantime, you can't stay here."

"How many spy boxes are there?"

"I found four. I don't think there's one on the deck, but there could be."

"Can't you just remove all of them?"

"I'd rather they stay in place while I find out who had reason to bug you. That way we can feed them false info if we need to. I'll put this one back in its original position."

"I'll be careful what I say, Travis. I'm here alone every night. It's not like I do a lot of talking. But I can't leave home. Cornell may try to call me again. If he does, I have to be here."

"Your landline is likely wiretapped, as well. Even if it isn't, they would be able to hear your conversation with Cornell. That might give them exactly what they're after."

This made no sense. Who would need to listen in to a conversation with Cornell? Not Travis, looking to arrest her son, or he'd never be telling her to move out. But if someone was this desperate to find Cornell, that might be why he was on the run. If she stayed, she might lead him into danger.

But danger from whom? This had to be linked to Angela Pointer. "Do you think Cornell and Angela ran away together because they were afraid of what her abusive boyfriend would do to them?"

"That's a possibility."

She was convinced Travis knew more than he was saying.

"Who knows about the phone call you got from Cornell?" he asked.

"You. Joni. Probably your brother. Joni tells Leif everything."

"Who else?"

Joni's words pounded in her head and in her heart like beating drums. *Trust Travis. Trust Travis. Trust Travis.*

Faith couldn't keep playing both ends against the middle. The situation had grown too dangerous. Forced to choose between Travis Dalton and the mysterious Georgio, she decided there was only one way to go.

"Georgio knows."

"Georgio Trosclair of the Passion Pit?"

She nodded.

"How would he?"

"I told him."

ANGER ERUPTED INSIDE TRAVIS. He slammed his right fist into his other palm while he tried to turn on his brain and turn off the fury and frustration.

"I told you to stay clear of him."

"He saw one of the flyers I put up. He called me and offered his help in finding Cornell. I couldn't turn that down."

"So he's the one who poisoned your mind against me. What part of *evil* and *dangerous* do you not understand, Faith? The bastard's the biggest drug smuggler in Texas, and nobody crosses him and lives to tell about it."

"Then why isn't he in jail?"

"Because no one lives to testify against him, either."

"Are you accusing him of murder?"

"Not directly. He has others do his dirty work for him."

Travis raked the hair back from his forehead. He hadn't expected things to heat up this fast, though he'd figured Georgio would find out that Travis was working with Faith to find Cornell. But even before that, Georgio had contacted Faith, so something else had changed.

"Let's take a walk," he said.

He let everything roll around in his mind as they walked side by side, but not touching. No more illusions of romance or lusty fantasies where Faith was concerned. He had to be all cop while he figured out a way to keep her and Cornell safe.

They took a walking trail that ran through her neighborhood, stopping at a bench in the shade of a gnarled oak tree.

He'd expected resistance, but Faith started talking the second they were seated. Her voice was unsteady, so the words spilled from her like water over a rocky creek bed.

The more she told him about her two meetings with Georgio, the madder Travis got. The man was definitely playing her, trying to discover exactly what she knew.

She finally took a deep breath, leaned against the back of the bench and stared into space. "None of this makes sense. Why would the dancers think Angela was murdered? And why is Georgio pretending to be helping me now when he'd refused to talk to me before?"

"I don't know, but right now we have to get you out of your house. How difficult would it be to take a few days off work?"

"I have some vacation time coming. I've been saving it so that I could spend it with Cornell when he comes home."

"Take it. You're going under unofficial protective custody."

"Is there such a thing?"

"There is now."

"Where will I stay?"

"Someplace where you'll be safe and near enough to the city that I can keep an eye on you."

Only one spot like that came to mind. A location where

his nightmares and resentments of the past would collide with the fears and pressures of the present. The last place he'd ever expected to spend even one night.

"I'll walk you back to your house, and I want you to go in and turn your TV or music up loud so that the sophisticated bugs won't pick up the packing sounds."

"What should I pack?"

"Jeans, shorts, T-shirts, boots if you have them, nothing fancy. Whatever you think you need on a ranch."

"What ranch?"

"The Dry Gulch."

CORNELL HELPED LOAD the last horse into the carrier, then wiped the sweat from his brow with his sleeve. He didn't understand half of what the Mexicans who were helping him said, but he understood enough to know they thought he was crazy for heading to the border with this load of smuggled goods.

More money for Georgio. More risk of arrest for Cornell. How long could this go on before one of the border patrol recognized him? How long before an agent figured out that the horses were not the only thing he was transporting into the U.S.?

Five trips. That was what Georgio had promised. The man lied as easily and with the same careless disregard as he manipulated lives. But no one crossed him. No one dared.

Cornell might.

What did he have to lose? Spend the rest of his life on the run or spend it behind bars? Killed by one of Georgio's thugs or facing a death sentence?

At least if he escaped Georgio's clutches he had a chance of staying alive. But never back in the U.S. Never would he return home. Never see his mother's face again.

He couldn't go running back to her, couldn't bear to see the pain in her eyes if she knew what he'd done.

He was eighteen, a man. Men fought wars at that age. Only Cornell didn't really feel like a man.

This time when he brushed away the sweat, his sleeve caught a couple salty tears. Showing that kind of nervous weakness would get him arrested for sure.

He pushed the Stetson back on his head and pretended to be the tough, long-haired, bearded cowboy that looked at him every morning in the mirror.

"Secure that door," he ordered. "Time to roll."

Maybe for the last time, if he could get his nerve up to make a run for it.

Chapter Ten

R.J. sat in the worn front-porch rocker, grateful for his neighbor's company. There was no one quite like Carolina Lambert to help him sort out a few things in his mind. Prettiest grandma he'd ever seen. Smart, too.

Carolina fitted one of the small flowered throw pillows behind her back as she settled in the creaky porch swing. "Do you have any idea why this change of heart with Travis?"

"Nope. I'm as confused as a golf ball on Astroturf."

"But he did say that he and Joni's friend Faith would be staying with you for a few days?"

"He asked me if I had room. Knows darn well I do. Got nothing but room in this rambling old house now that Leif and Joni moved into their own cottage."

"But you're never really alone these days. Your family is coming home."

"Some of them are taking their own good time about it. If they don't get a move on, it'll be too late to be any good. I've already outlived my oncologist's prognosis. Brain tumor's as stubborn as a mule in clover."

"But not as stubborn as you. And your methods for getting your family to move back to the ranch were a bit underhanded."

"Nothing underhanded about it. They want my money,

they dance to my fiddle playing, at least as long as I'm this side of the red Texas clay. 'Sides, I got the idea from you."

"I suggested you leave them the ranch. I never mentioned letting them think you were dead and then showing up at the reading of your own will."

R.J. chuckled. "Sure was worth it seeing the looks on their faces when I walked in. Thought my oldest son, Jake, was going to swallow his tongue."

"Speaking of Jake, have you heard from him lately?"

"Yep. Still complaining about the terms of the will. Thinks I'm a conniving son of a bitch."

Carolina smiled. "Wonder where he'd get an idea like that."

"Don't you start on me, too."

"Wouldn't dream of it."

"More likely he's been listening to his mother. Pretty as a red heifer in a flower bed, that one. Stole my heart the second I met her."

Never gave the dad-blasted thing back, either. Not even when she'd left him.

Not that he hadn't loved all his wives in his own way. Just something about the first time… Now he was getting sentimental. Never did that when he was younger and healthy.

"I remember Joni saying that the best man and the maid of honor had never met before the wedding," Carolina said. "They must have hit it off fast if they're taking a mini vacation together."

"I got the feeling this is more business than pleasure," R.J. said.

"Police business."

He nodded. "I talked to Leif last night. He says Travis

is helping Faith find her teenage son, who went missing months ago. Never a dull moment around the Dry Gulch."

"I'm so sorry to hear that. Faith's heart must be breaking. I'll be praying that Travis finds him safe and alive."

"You pray about everything."

"Everything that matters, including you. And whatever brings Travis here, at least you'll get the opportunity to connect with him."

"I'll see him. Not so sure about connecting. He sounded more guarded than friendly."

"He can't be any more reluctant to have a relationship with you than Adam and Leif were, and look how well that worked out."

"You're right. Reckon two out of six adult kids forgiving me for being a lousy dad is better than I deserve."

"Forgiving is not related to deserving. And call me an optimist, R. J. Dalton, but I have this sneaking suspicion that all six of your children will at least make a visit within the next few months. If not, it's their loss."

"I won't be holding my breath for Jake to show up. If he does, it will be to harangue me." R.J. scratched his jaw, thinking that even his face felt unfamiliar now. He'd lost thirty pounds since the doc had handed him the death sentence.

The only real pleasure he had was having Adam and his family and Leif and Joni around. Those two adorable twin girls of Leif's were a pure joy.

"I'd best be going," Carolina said. "I'm on my way to my Bible-study class and just wanted to drop off some of the vegetable-beef soup I made this morning."

"Appreciate that. You know how I love that soup. Rich, beautiful and you cook. Don't know how you keep the men from breaking down your door."

"I keep my shotgun loaded."

R.J. hooted and slapped his hand against his knee. "That'll keep out the riffraff."

"You know that Hugh was the love of my life, R.J. There's not a man in Texas who can fill his shoes."

But Hugh was dead and Carolina was much too young to crawl into bed alone every night. "No need to fill Hugh's shoes," R.J. said. "Get a man who's got his own boots."

"It would never be the same."

"No," he agreed. "But that don't mean it can't be good. Growing old alone can get mighty lonely."

Carolina rose from the porch swing, walked over and laid one of her graceful hands over his ruddy, wrinkled one. "Don't you worry about me, R.J. I'll never be alone as long as I have my family and my memories. You're not alone, either. And now you have another son on his way home."

"Yeah. Stay tuned. I'll let you know how that goes."

"You do that." She bent over and kissed him on his cheek.

He resisted the urge to give her a harmless pinch on her shapely bottom. She was too much a lady for his antics. So he merely watched and appreciated the view as she walked down the front steps and to her car.

He was courting the grim reaper, but he wasn't dead yet.

"ARE YOU SURE this is necessary, Travis? I feel awkward staying in your father's house with him suffering from a brain tumor, especially since he barely knows me."

"Too late to have second thoughts now. We're less than five miles from the ranch and I already told him we were on our way."

Besides, Travis was having enough second thoughts for both of them. He'd fought to push his resentment toward R.J. aside years ago. You took what life handed you and you ran with it. It was called survival.

But with every mile, the memories he'd stashed away became more vivid. He'd left the hell behind him, but the images would never disappear entirely.

Faith tugged on the restraining band of her seat belt and turned toward him. "I thought you and R.J. barely spoke."

"Hopefully, that won't change much in the next few days."

"I can see why you'd feel some residual bitterness," she said. "I can't imagine being farmed out to foster homes when your own father didn't take you in after your mother's death."

So his past was common knowledge. "Did Leif tell you that?"

"Joni. She says relations between Leif and R.J. were so strained at first, she feared Leif would never feel any kind of connection with him. And now he and Joni are building a house on Dry Gulch land."

"I'm not Leif."

"I've noticed," Faith said. "Cop versus attorney. Big difference, but you look like a man who'd be at home on a ranch. You have that natural cowboy swagger."

"Is that bad?"

"You wear the attitude well." She smiled in spite of the situation.

Unfortunately, Faith didn't leave it at that and let the subject of R.J. die.

"Joni says R.J. has lots of regrets about the way he lived his life."

"Dying reprobates usually do, or so I've heard."

"Joni didn't know the old R.J., but she really likes the man he is now. She's thrilled that he and Leif are finally working things out between them."

Time to change the subject, Travis decided as he turned onto the narrow county road that led to the ranch.

"Let's go over again what I need you to do and not do while you're staying at the ranch."

Faith rolled her eyes. "Isn't that overkill? You drilled it into me before we ever left Dallas."

"I thought I'd drilled it into your head to stay away from Georgio, too, and look how that turned out."

"Point made. I'm not supposed to tell anyone that I'm staying at the Dry Gulch Ranch. But do you really think that whoever bugged my house is going to try to track me down?"

"Yep. I do. Georgio is not one to be deterred by a small inconvenience like you not coming home after work."

"You really are convinced that he's the one who had the house bugged, aren't you?"

"Unless you've got a stalker or jealous lover you're keeping secret."

"No stalkers. No lovers, jealous or otherwise."

The no-lovers assurance was the only thing about this he liked. The one thing that shouldn't matter to him at all.

"Georgio feeds you a line of bull, says he'll take over the search for Cornell and warns you not to talk to the cops. Then your house is bugged while he makes sure you're not at home to get in the way. Doesn't take a detective to figure that one out."

She shifted and stared out the window. "I don't doubt you, but it's still hard to digest all of this. Georgio seemed so sincere."

"He's sincerely evil and manipulative and used to having things go his way. Take my word for that and don't say anything to give him a clue where you are or that you're with me."

"I'm sure he'll never guess that I'm at your father's ranch."

Travis found that hard to believe himself. The closer he got to the ranch, the stronger the temptation to turn around and find somewhere else to take Faith.

But he couldn't be with her every second, and she'd never be alone at the ranch. Adam, R.J., a wrangler named Corky and a couple of young wranglers from Canada Adam had hired on to work for the summer would all be there. They could handle trouble if it popped up, not that Travis expected it to. Georgio limited his witnesses.

Adam's wife and twin daughters would be on the Dry Gulch as well, so Faith would have female company to hopefully keep her spirits from bottoming out.

He slowed and turned off the county road onto the ranch blacktop. The metal gate was closed. He stopped and shifted into Park.

"I'll get it," Faith said, opening her door and jumping out before he could beat her to the task. She was graceful as a doe, her dark hair dancing about her slender shoulders, her hips swaying as she walked to the gate and then unlatched it.

Travis's mind battled with his libido. There was no doubt which was winning as she swung open the gate and waited for him on the other side.

Worst part of it all was that his infatuation with her went far deeper than just physical attraction. It was her vulnerability, her toughness when she looked as soft as spring hay, her commitment to her son. Hell, it was everything about her.

Five minutes later they arrived at the old ranch house. The structure looked years older in the glaring sun than it had in the glittering lights that had illuminated the area on Leif's wedding night. The shutters needed replacing. The paint was fading.

Yet somehow the pots of blooming flowers, the worn rockers and the colorful pillows tossed onto the wooden porch swing gave the place a homey feel.

But it wasn't Travis's home.

Hadn't been since he was much too young to remember it, and would never be again. Leif, Adam and the others could do as they chose, but Travis wasn't about to grovel for a share of the inheritance that should have come automatically to him.

Even if it had, he wasn't sure he'd have accepted it. R.J. hadn't been there when Travis was all alone and desperately needed a father. As far as he was concerned, R.J. was no kin to him.

Travis got out of the truck and rounded the front of it on his way to open Faith's door. The sound of horse hooves slapping against the dry earth caught his attention. He turned and watched R.J approach on a beautiful filly.

Atop the magnificent animal, R.J. looked much more virile than the frail, confused man Travis had helped into the house after the reception Saturday night. Leif had said he had his good days and his bad days. Apparently, this was the former.

Faith got out of the car and walked over to where he was dismounting.

"Sorry I wasn't here when you arrived," R.J. said. "Be a shame to waste a day like this inside, so I took Miss Dazzler for a ride. Left the door unlocked, though. Always do."

"No problem," Faith said. "We just arrived."

"I'll hitch Miss Dazzler to the porch railing and then call Corky to come ride her to the barn and get her unsaddled."

"I can do that for you," Travis offered. Might as well make an attempt at friendliness, since they were going to be sharing a roof for a few days.

"Appreciate the offer," R.J. said. "But Corky can handle Miss Dazzler while you two fill me in on what brought you here. Not that you're not welcome, whatever it is. Lord knows I got the room. Place is so empty and lonesome at night, even ghosts avoid it."

Faith took R.J.'s arm as they climbed the steps. Travis lingered behind for a few seconds, attempting to come to grips with the fact that no matter why he was here, he was about to reopen a cask full of old wounds.

His cell phone vibrated before he reached the top step. John Patterson. An old friend who had worked for the DPD before taking a position with Border Patrol.

Travis took the call. "What's up, John?"

"You know that missing son of a friend you asked me to check out? Cornell Ashburn?"

"Yeah. Did you locate him?"

"Yes and no."

"What does that mean?"

"He's in the area, but he managed to get away from my agents. It's a long story, and I'd rather not go into it on the phone. But I can tell you this. Cornell Ashburn is not just some innocent runaway. There will be a warrant out for his arrest by morning."

Chapter Eleven

Travis swallowed the curses that flew to his throat. The news from John Patterson hadn't shocked him, but it meant he'd have to destroy Faith's trust in her son—the only thing getting her through this.

"I'll try to be there before that happens," Travis said.

There was a short period of silence. "Don't come to the office. Just give me a call," John said. "I'll meet you someplace where we can talk—off the record. Officially, you and I haven't spoken."

"Got it."

When Travis broke the connection, he realized that both R.J. and Faith were staring at him expectantly.

Faith's expression was grim and her smooth hands were knotted into tight fists, the strain mirrored in her dark, expressive eyes. "Was that phone call about Cornell?"

Travis hesitated, determining how to handle this. If he lied to her, she'd find out eventually, anyway. The lie would break their fragile bonds of trust. It might even backfire completely and send her running back to Georgio for help.

"It was, wasn't it?" she repeated.

Travis nodded, dreading the questions that would follow.

"Has someone located him?" Her voice trembled.

"No, but there appears to be a credible lead."

She exhaled slowly. "Finally. Is he in Texas?"

"Laredo, or at least that's where I have to go to meet my source and follow up on the lead."

"Sounds vague," R.J. interjected. "Who is this source of yours, anyway? Is he in law enforcement?"

Travis stopped himself from blurting out that this was none of R.J.'s business. In a way it was his business now. Bringing Faith here for protection had changed the rules.

"He's a friend," Travis said, not giving anything else away.

"I don't care who he is," Faith said, "as long as he can help me find my son."

"Nothing's guaranteed," Travis reminded her, knowing that if John was right, finding Cornell would dump a whole new set of worries and heartbreak on Faith.

"How far is it to Laredo?" she asked.

"Somewhere around five hundred miles, give or take a detour or two," R.J. answered.

"Then just a short flight," she declared, excitement building in her voice. "Planes fly out of Dallas every few minutes. Surely there's one to Laredo tonight. All we have to do is call and see which ones have seats available."

"Seats?"

"I'm going with you," she said. "I'd go crazy just sitting around here waiting."

How the devil had he bungled this up so bad? "Not a good idea," Travis said.

"Why not?" Faith demanded.

Because she wouldn't like what she'd learn. Because they might find her son behind bars.

"All I have is a lead, Faith. It may take days to track it fully. You'll be a lot more comfortable waiting here."

"I'm going with you," she said firmly.

R.J. scratched his chin. "Might wind up no more than chasing a hawk's shadow, Faith. If I were you, I'd let Travis do the legwork. He's used to it."

At least this time R.J. was interfering in Travis's favor.

Faith shook her head. "It's been ten months. Ten months of tears and heartbreak and fear that never lets go. If there's even a chance this will lead to finding Cornell, I deserve to be there."

Travis gave up the argument, but he still had no intention of taking her with him.

"I'll check with the airlines," he said.

"If we can't get a flight, we can drive," Faith urged.

"Take you half the night to get there in a car," R.J. stated.

"But we'd be there. I'd rather be driving than just waiting," Faith insisted. "You said yourself the clue is credible, Travis. We shouldn't waste time. We can take turns driving while the other sleeps. We'd be in Laredo by morning."

"You'd be plumb tuckered out," R.J. said, still doing the arguing for Travis. Not that there was any way he'd wait until morning.

Travis moved to the front door. "Let's talk inside."

"Good idea," R.J. agreed. "Matilda was making a fresh pot of coffee when I left for my short ride. She does that every afternoon. Has her a cup and then heads home. Once you get settled, that just might hit the spot." He opened the door and led the way.

"I hope I'm not putting you out too much," Faith said. "If we'd had any idea we'd be catching a plane tonight, we wouldn't have had to bother you at all."

"Never a bother having a pretty woman around. And God knows I've got the room, what with Adam and

Hadley and the girls in their own place, and Leif and Joni off honeymooning. This house is as lonely as a church pew on Saturday night."

He should have thought of that before running off on all his wives. Travis stopped behind Faith as R.J. flung open a door off the hallway.

"Plenty more guest rooms upstairs," R.J. said, "but this is the best of the bunch. Bought a new mattress for the old four-poster. Joni and my other daughter-in-law, Hadley, did the rest of the sprucing up."

Faith stepped inside. "It's lovely," she said, though it was obvious her thoughts were still on getting to Laredo and the prospect of finding her son.

Their only hope was that John Patterson had the wrong man. John never did.

Faith turned to R.J. "Do you have a computer we can use to check flights?"

"There's a laptop on the desk in the family room. We've even got wireless in the house now. Adam's bringing the Dry Gulch up to snuff with all that tech stuff. I swear he can tell you how many bulls got lucky last night with just a couple of double clicks."

Travis seriously doubted that and didn't want to even think about getting lucky, since he was certain he wouldn't be.

"I have my laptop with me," he said. "I'll check for flights."

"Good idea," R.J. said. "Password is *NOTLAD,* all caps. That's *Dalton* spelled backward. Had to find something I can remember. My memory being what it is these days, I can't always recall something as simple as that."

Travis turned on the computer and began to scan for available flights. As he suspected, the last direct flight out tonight left in forty-five minutes. No way could he make that. There were a few later flights, but they went around the moon to get there and didn't make it until tomorrow morning, anyway.

Faith was hanging over his shoulder, so he didn't have to explain the situation to her. What he needed was to get her out of the room while he made a call and booked a charter flight. One that would cost him a small fortune and get him to Laredo as quickly as possible.

He pushed back from the antique mahogany desk where he'd been working. "We need to talk, Faith."

TRAVIS LOOKED EVERY bit the classic hero, from the rugged planes of his face to the piercing stare that seemed to see right through her. But tonight there was no smile to add that mischievous flair to his lips. No swagger to his step once he'd taken that phone call on the porch.

Yet even with tension so thick it seemed to squeeze the air from the room, she was drawn to him in a way she'd never been drawn to any man. More than sensual. Far more than physical. A mysterious bond that made her ache to trust him.

In spite of that, she knew he was holding back, keeping things from her. Protecting—or manipulating? Either way, she wouldn't be humored and kept in the dark.

She walked over and sat on the edge of the bed, the new mattress barely giving beneath her weight. "We do need to talk, Travis, but honestly. I admit I'm naive, especially where Cornell is concerned. But I'm not stupid."

"I never thought for a second that you were."

"But you're treating me like I am."

He stood and began to pace the room, avoiding eye contact. "How do you mean?"

"You said there was a credible lead, but I didn't hear any relief in your voice—not when you were talking to the caller or to me and R.J. Your words say one thing, your body language something completely opposite."

"Good thing the suspects I interrogate don't read me the way you do."

"What did the caller really tell you, Travis?"

"You're not totally off base," he admitted. "But I didn't lie to you, Faith. There is a good chance that Cornell is in or near Laredo, perhaps on the Mexican side of the border."

"What else did he say?"

"You're not going to give up until I level with you, are you?"

"No, but I can handle this. I'm tougher than I look."

"I'm figuring that out." He started to sit down beside her, but then walked over to the desk chair and pulled it over instead. He sat facing her, inches away, a pained look glazing his dark eyes.

"John, that's the caller's first name. I'd like to leave the rest anonymous for now. Anyway, he says there will be a warrant out for Cornell's arrest before morning."

Her temper erupted. "What are the charges?"

"John didn't say. He didn't want to talk over the phone, but my guess is that they have to do with smuggling drugs across the border."

"Why would you guess that?"

"Because of Georgio's involvement in this. If he's using your son to run drugs, then it would explain why he bugged your house once he found out Cornell was trying to get in touch with you."

"You're wrong," she said. "Cornell would never get involved in smuggling—unless…"

"Go on," Travis encouraged.

"Unless he's being blackmailed by Georgio. Only I

can't imagine what he could have done that would give Georgio grounds for blackmail."

Faith knew what Travis was thinking, the same thing she'd be thinking if this was someone else taking about her son. That she was a mother who refused to think her boy capable of committing a crime, even though he'd clearly had a life he'd kept secret from her. A lover who was an erotic dancer. That he was possibly the father of a child, a grandson or granddaughter she'd never seen or rocked to sleep or sung a lullaby to.

A suffocating ache swelled in Faith's chest. In her mind, Cornell was still a child. Had she clung too tightly? Had she needed him to need her so badly that she'd blinded herself to what was going on with him? Had he turned to Georgio instead of her?

And now…

"The young men whose murders you've been investigating, Travis. Do you think it's possible Georgio had them killed for crossing him?"

Travis reached over and took her hands in his. He massaged her palms with his thumbs. "I don't think there's anything Georgio is not capable of, Faith."

"Then if he thinks Cornell is about to be arrested, he might go after my son himself, to keep him from implicating him under interrogation."

It had taken her a few minutes to come to this conclusion, but Travis would have thought it the second he took that call. "And to think I almost played right into Georgio's hands."

"But you didn't," Travis said.

"We have to find Cornell before Georgio does," Faith said, a new sense of urgency making her more determined than ever. "We have to get to Laredo at once. Charter a plane. I'll find a way to pay for it."

"I can take care of the flight, Faith. But you just heard me explain how dangerous this could be. I can't take you with me. Surely you understand that now."

"I only understand one thing. We have to find my son and there is no time to waste. And I will be going either with you, Travis, or on my own."

"You make it hard for a man to protect you, Faith Ashburn."

"But it means a lot that you want to," she admitted.

She wanted to say more. Tell him that when this was over, how much she'd love to be held in his strong, protective arms and taste his tempting, heroic lips.

But first they had to find Cornell. She had the needs of a woman, but the heart of a mother.

THE JARRING RING of the doorbell interrupted the fourth phone call Travis had made in search of a charter service that could get the two of them to Laredo tonight without swallowing his meager checking account. He heard deep male voices in the house mingling with R.J.'s weaker one.

Hopefully, the company would leave before Travis was forced to interact with them. He had too much on his mind for small talk.

"No plane available before morning," he said, reiterating what the woman on the other end of the phone had just told him.

"I'm sorry, but there's a major international energy conference in town and people have been jetting in and out all week," she added.

"What about your turboprop planes?"

"Have one that might be available about 1:00 a.m., but I'll have to see if I can locate a pilot. Regulations won't let the guy piloting it now clock any more hours without a significant break."

"Okay. I may get back to you."

But first Travis would get back to John Patterson and ask to be informed immediately if and when Cornell was arrested. If he was behind bars, not getting there before tomorrow would pose no problems, though Travis was certain Faith wouldn't see it that way.

Travis massaged the back of his neck, a futile effort to relieve the ever-building tension.

Faith put a hand on his shoulder. "No luck?"

"Not yet."

"Cornell, about to be arrested. I can't bear the thought of him behind bars and yet I wish he would be. Then I could at least talk to him, know he's safe. We could get this horrible misunderstanding straightened out and I could take him home."

As always the desperation in her voice turned Travis inside out. He longed to hold her close and whisper that everything would be all right, but it would be an empty promise. And once she was in his arms, with her soft body pressed into his, comfort wouldn't be the only thing on his mind.

He wanted to kiss her, had wanted to since the night he first laid eyes on her in the Passion Pit, though he hadn't admitted that to himself then. Now the desire was entangled with his need to keep her safe and help her find her son.

The urgency should have cooled his sensual cravings. Instead, it was making them worse.

He heard R.J.'s scuffling footfalls outside the guest room, followed by taps on the door.

Travis walked over and flung it open.

"I got a couple of guys in the kitchen I'd like you to meet, Travis."

Not the best of times for being sociable, but Travis

could use a cup of coffee and a break from the lustful urges that were starting to pummel his senses.

R.J. leaned against the doorframe. "You're welcome to join us, too, Faith. I think you'll be interested in what the Lamberts have to say."

Reluctantly, Travis closed his computer and followed Faith and R.J. to the kitchen.

One of the men was refilling his coffee cup. The other was sitting at the table, his elbows resting on an unfolded map of Texas. Both looked the part of real ranchers. Tanned. Lean and muscular. Dressed in jeans and Western shirts and wearing work-worn cowboy boots.

R.J. took care of the introductions. Tague and Damien Lambert. The names sounded familiar. Perhaps Leif had mentioned them.

"I don't mean to pry into your business, but I hear you're in a hurry to get to Laredo," Damien said once Faith and Travis had coffees in hand.

"We were hoping to get there tonight," Travis said. "Not having much luck with that, though." He let it go at that, not willing to get into details with a couple of strangers.

"We have a new four-seater Piper we use mostly for ranch business," Damien said. "It's not as comfortable as the corporate jets owned by Lambert Oil, but it'll get you to Laredo with no problems and it's available. All we'd have to do is fill it with fuel."

The Lamberts, one of the richest oil and ranching families in Texas. No wonder the names had sounded familiar. "Do you have a pilot?" Travis asked, suddenly fully engaged.

Tague grinned. "Me. And it just so happens I have a few hours to kill."

"Are you offering to fly Faith and me to Laredo tonight?" Travis asked.

"Yeah, if you're interested. Only problem is I'll have to fly straight from Laredo to A&M in the morning for a seminar I'm leading on innovative breeding ideas."

"No problem there," Travis said. "We can find a commercial flight back. It's just getting there that's urgent."

"Then I guess it's settled." Tague lifted and tipped his cup as if it were a crystal flute and they were making toasts.

Problem solved almost too easily, Travis decided. Easy always made him suspicious. "What's the charge?"

"No charge. Just call it a neighborly gesture."

"A very thoughtful gesture," Travis said, shocked that R.J., a womanizing boozer who hadn't bothered to keep in touch with any of his own children for most of his life, was such good friends with a family as socially elite as the Lamberts.

"R.J. says you're looking at some real trouble that needs immediate attention," Damien said. "If we can help, it would be a downright sin not to."

"Plus, we've all been there," Tague said. "When trouble hits, you need family and friends. No questions asked, by the way. No explanations required. It's the cowboy way of doing business."

Travis knew the cowboy way. It wasn't so different from the cop code. But none of his cop friends owned prop planes.

"If you're sure you don't mind, Faith and I will definitely take you up on your offer."

"We're sure," Tague said.

They worked out the details over a second cup of coffee. Two hours later they had taken off and were headed toward Laredo.

GEORGIO STARED AT the traffic ahead, cursing the other drivers, seething with anger. Things were going south at the speed of light. Somehow Faith Ashburn was behind all this. He should have given the word to have Cornell killed the second he'd heard that the mixed-up kid had called his mother.

No, he should have had him killed the first night Faith had showed up at the Passion Pit. The woman had always been trouble. Too gutsy. Too determined. A pit bull without a leash.

Instead he'd stupidly found her amusing, been impressed by all that motherly concern. A quality his own mother had sadly lacked.

Georgio had figured that after a few months, Faith would grow weary and leave the search for her son to the police. Cops, or any other law-enforcement officials for that matter, had never been much of a challenge for Georgio. Either they were too tied up by rules and regulation to be effective, or they could be bought.

Travis Dalton was the exception. He and his latest partner, Reno Vargas, had dogged Georgio constantly for the past eighteen months, had been in and out of his clubs more often than any of his paying clientele. Asking questions. Making Georgio's customers and employees nervous.

And now Cornell had screwed up royally. There was a warrant out for his arrest. He was on the run—not only from the hapless border agents, but apparently from Georgio, as well. There had been no contact.

The kid couldn't possibly think Georgio wouldn't know about the incident. Or maybe he could. Cornell was naive enough to buy into everything Georgio had told him to this point. Naive and desperate.

In spite of that, Georgio had started to like Cornell. He'd even anticipated a few romps with Faith.

Too bad that both Cornell and his mother would have to die. Georgio liked his problems wrapped up neatly, and there was one thing you could always count on with corpses. They never squealed or testified.

Chapter Twelve

Faith stared straight ahead at the string of red taillights that stretched out in front of their rented sedan. Her muscles were stiff from the constant tension. The lining of her stomach felt as if it had been smeared with acid.

She stretched and pulled one foot onto the seat with her. "How much farther to the truck stop where we're supposed to meet John?"

"Ten more miles."

"Did you ever tell him that I'd be with you?"

"No, but there's something else I should tell you. John is not just a friend. He's a border-patrol agent."

"Why didn't you tell me that originally?"

"He's talking to me unofficially. That's why we're meeting at the truck stop. I'm not sure he'll be as open if I show up with you."

Her frustrations swelled yet again. "Cornell is my son. I have every right to know why he's being arrested."

"I'd still like to talk to John alone first."

"So I just sit in the car?"

"No. I'm not comfortable with that."

"So what's the plan?"

"You go in first," Travis said. "Take a seat and order from the menu, even if it's just coffee. I'll come in a few minutes later and go sit by John. After that, I'll just have to play this by ear."

"I don't see why you get to call all the shots, Travis."

"Because I'm a cop and you—"

The ringing of her phone interrupted his answer. She checked the caller ID.

Unavailable.

Faith's breath caught. Her heart pounded. "It must be Cornell," she whispered. "Hello?"

She heard breathing on the line, but no voice.

"Cornell. Cornell."

"Mrs. Ashburn."

A woman's voice. Low. Shaky. Faith took a deep breath and bit back tears as dashed hope churned in her stomach.

"Yes," she said. "Who's calling?"

"You don't know me, but my name is Angela."

Faith's heart skipped a beat. "Angela Pointer?"

"Yes, ma'am. How do you know about me?"

"From emails found on Cornell's computer. Have you talked to Cornell? Do you know where he is?"

"I don't know where he is. He wouldn't say, but I did hear from him. He's in trouble, Mrs. Ashburn. Bad trouble."

"What kind of trouble?" If she pretended not to know anything, perhaps Angela would tell her the full truth.

"I can't say. But he wants you to know that no matter what you hear, he loves you. And he's sorry for all he's done."

"What has he done, Angela? What has he done that he would need to apologize to me for?"

"He's broken the law. He wants you to know that it's all his doing, and he doesn't want you to get involved. Don't try to find him."

"If Cornell broke the law, he had to have a very good reason. I can help him, Angela. I'm with a cop right now who's on his side. I just have to know where to find him."

"He doesn't want you to look for him, Mrs. Ashburn. He loves you. Just know that."

"I do, but I have to find—"

Angela broke the connection. Faith held tight to the phone, willing her to pick up again, but the phone stayed silent. Her one link to Cornell had vaporized into thin air.

"I take it that was Angela Pointer," Travis said.

"Yes. She refused to tell me, but I'm sure she knows where Cornell is. We have to track down that number."

"I'll call the precinct and have someone trace the call. What did Angela tell you?"

Faith shared the gist of the message, new fears forming as she did. "I think Angela is turning against Cornell, if she was ever with him. She worked for Georgio. It makes sense that they were both involved in Cornell's disappearance."

"Anything's possible," Travis agreed.

The possibilities made Faith nauseated. If she was right, this conniving, lying woman might be the mother of her grandchild—a child that might never be part of Faith's life.

Memories flooded her, of the first time she'd held Cornell in her arms. She'd worried that she wouldn't know what to do, feared that she might not even like the baby who would soon take over her life.

But then he'd wrapped his tiny fingers around one of hers and wrapped himself around her heart. That the tiny infant could be a living, breathing being, part of her, part of his father, had seemed like a miracle almost beyond comprehension.

At that moment, she'd become a real mother.

She remembered his first seizure. Faith had walked into his room and found him writhing on the floor, his eyes rolled back in his head. And then there was the night she and Melvin had stayed at his bedside all night, crying, praying, afraid he wouldn't make it until morning. Each breath had been a struggle—for Cornell and for them.

That same sick panic that she was about to lose him was taking over again.

She looked up as Travis slowed and then pulled into the parking lot of a truck stop. The big rigs were parked in the back. A few cars, two pickup trucks and a cluster of motorcycles lined the front.

Travis parked near the front door. "I'll call my partner while you go inside," he said. "I want to get someone tracing that phone number pronto."

"What does your friend look like?"

"Mid-fifties, receding hairline, salt-and-pepper hair. Wearing a red plaid shirt."

She realized then that he'd already spotted the man through the wide, dirt-smeared windows. She nodded, then opened the door and stepped out onto the pavement.

A few seconds later, she walked right by the secretive border-patrol agent. There was a gun at his hip. No doubt loaded and ready to fire.

A gun that he would undoubtedly use to kill her son if it came to that.

"Find Angela Pointer," Travis said once he'd filled Reno in on the latest phone call from her. "If we do, I'm almost positive she could lead us to Cornell."

"I'm working on it," Reno said. "I've also put a tail 24/7 on Georgio. If Cornell screwed up smuggling a cache of drugs for him, Georgio will do his best to keep Cornell from being arrested and interrogated."

"Exactly," Travis agreed. "And we both know what he's willing to do to make sure no one involves him in his own dirty work. I figure he's already been in touch with Cornell and is calling all the shots."

"Like a possible execution, gangster-style. Do you need me in Laredo?"

"Not at the present. I'd rather have you on top of things in Dallas. Finding Cornell is getting more critical by the second."

"Right. Give me a call once you talk to Patterson."

"Will do. Later."

Travis pocketed his phone, got out of the car and went inside. He glanced at Faith and then sidled into a chair opposite John.

John pushed an empty plate away. "Fast trip."

"Friend with a plane."

"Ah. Moving up in the world. I heard you were in for a big inheritance."

"Where did you hear that?"

"Word gets around. Money and part interest in a ranch was the way I heard it."

"Don't believe everything you hear."

The waitress came over and refilled John's cup. "What can I get you?"

"Hamburger's good," John said. "Onion rings are even better." He wiped his mouth on a paper napkin.

"I've eaten," Travis said. "Just coffee for me."

John waited until the waitress was out of earshot. "Exactly what is your connection to Cornell Ashburn?"

"His mother is best friends with my new sister-in-law." That was a fact, though it barely scratched the surface of the truth.

"This news is not going to make her happy."

"No doubt about that, but she's so desperate to find him that an arrest might be a relief."

"I can understand that. I've got a sixteen-year-old son myself. A good kid but a bit of a rebel. I worry about him all the time."

"I'd worry he wasn't your son if he didn't have a bit of a rebel in him."

John grinned and then went right back to business.

"The warrant for Cornell's arrest has been issued and the case is officially open, so I can fully level with you now."

"Hit me with it."

"Cornell has been towing a horse trailer across the border every few weeks for months. He picks up two to three horses and brings them into America."

"Are the horses stolen?"

"No. He's been stopped more than once in the past. Paperwork is always in order. They are legitimate sales and animals have passed inspection. But you know how it is. We're always suspicious that a young man crossing the border at frequent intervals may be into drug smuggling."

"You must have found proof that he was."

"No. Even the dogs never found a trace of drugs in that horse trailer or the pickup truck he was driving."

"Until today?"

John shook his head and waited as the waitress set a white mug of steaming coffee in front of Travis.

She leaned over, revealing a seductive glimpse of cleavage. "We have some great apple pie. Sure you don't want a piece to go with that java?"

Travis waved her off. "Not tonight, thanks.... So why the warrant?" he asked when the waitress had left.

"We were anonymously tipped off today that there was a hidden compartment built into the floor of the horse trailer. I ordered in some extra agents to check out the tip."

"If not drugs, what did you find?"

"Solid-gold religious icons and other statues and jeweled relics believed stolen from a church in Peru over the last few years. The stolen goods were estimated to be worth billions."

"Son of a bitch. Georgio Trosclair has apparently branched out into new, even more lucrative endeavors."

John's eyebrows arched. "I never mentioned Georgio."

"Then I should tell you the rest of the story. But first, if you found stolen relics in the horse trailer, why didn't you take Cornell into custody then?"

"A question I've asked everybody at the scene. He slipped away even before they found the contraband. It was as if he knew they'd been tipped off that it was there."

"Maybe he was the one who supplied the tip."

"I considered that," John said.

Travis filled him in on the details of Cornell's disappearance, his connection with Angela Pointer and Georgio's recent attempt to reach out to Faith, culminating with her house being bugged.

"That explains a lot," John said. "I figured there was no way Cornell Ashburn had masterminded and carried this out on his own. I wish I had known that sooner, but we didn't even know Cornell's real name until we realized the ID he carried today was fake. It still might have taken days to identify him if you hadn't sent that picture to me personally."

And by that time, Georgio would likely have found Cornell first. He still might. The gory reality of that pushed a new wave of adrenaline through Travis's veins.

"We need every available resource dedicated to finding Cornell," he urged. "Rangers, state police, border patrol and local cops. You know what it means if Georgio gets to him first."

"I'm on it the second we leave here," John said. "And I need to talk to Cornell's mother. What's the best way to reach her?"

"Through me." Travis turned, caught Faith's eye and motioned her over.

"Just a friend of your sister-in-law," John said, clearly not believing him. "You failed to mention she was a knockout."

"Is she? I never noticed."

"Right."

The kidding around stopped the second Travis introduced Faith to John. The situation was dead serious.

An hour after meeting Travis's friend, Faith was practically numb, still fighting off shock at the ludicrous accusations against Cornell. She dropped her handbag to the sofa, barely noticing the roomy suite in the recently renovated motel John Patterson had recommended.

Patterson had spoken of a man. Cornell was just a kid, a teen beginning his senior year in high school when he'd disappeared. Listening to the accusations Patterson had spouted so coldly had been difficult. Believing them was impossible.

Yet John Patterson believed them. She suspected Travis did, as well.

"It's been a long day," Travis said.

"Only a day. It seems weeks since I met Georgio for lunch."

"You should probably get some sleep. You take the bed. I'll take the sofa."

"Or we could toss a coin for it," she suggested.

"No. The couch is fine with me. I never sleep much when I'm working on a case."

"Aren't you always working on a case?"

"Yep. Sleep is overrated."

"I'm pretty sure I won't sleep tonight, either," she said.

Travis dropped to the sofa and propped his feet on the wooden coffee table. "Want to talk?"

"I may not make sense. I'm bewildered, unable to relate to the person John Patterson says is my son."

"I can understand that. Talking about it might help."

"I don't see how." She sank to the sofa beside him. "I know it's hard to understand if you don't have a son of your own, but I know this is not what it seems. If Cornell was driving that horse trailer, he either didn't know about the contraband or was somehow forced to do it."

"Tell me about the Cornell you know, Faith."

"You think I'm just a prejudiced mother, don't you?"

"I think you're an amazing woman who loves her son very much. I had a mother like that—or so I've been told. I don't remember much about her. You've probably heard that she died of cancer about the time I started school."

"She'd be proud of you," Faith said. How could she not? He was tough, a man's man. Yet he was also protective and gentle and…

And she was falling hard for him. Crazy to feel this when her life was in chaos and her heart was breaking. But she'd love nothing more than to find refuge in the protective warmth of his strong arms.

"I don't know where to start talking about Cornell," she said.

"Start wherever you like."

She closed her eyes for a few seconds, letting the thoughts of happier times creep into her consciousness. "I was seventeen and pregnant when I married Melvin

Ashburn. He was two years older, out of high school and working for his dad in the construction business."

"Awful young to start a family. Of course, I'm almost thirty-nine and have never even gotten married. But that's a topic for another time."

She wondered if that was his way of warning her not to get any romantic ideas where he was concerned. It was a warning her heart should heed.

"We were young," she agreed, "so I guess it wasn't so surprising that once Cornell was born, Melvin felt trapped. He hung out with his friends, drinking and carousing."

"And you stayed home with Cornell?"

"I did. He was my life. I marveled at each new thing he did. The first words. The first steps. And somehow the marriage survived far longer than the teenage hormone-induced lust we'd been sure was the real thing."

"How did Cornell react to the divorce?"

"He took it hard, the way any kid does when his father walks out. He felt as if his dad had abandoned him instead of me."

"What kind of father was Melvin after the divorce?"

"The kind who was seldom around, the same as before the divorce. But he did breeze in on occasion and take Cornell on exciting trips. And he was there with me when Cornell almost died from his mysterious illness."

Travis pulled his feet from the coffee table and turned to face her. "A divorce, an illness that almost killed him, a seizure disorder and the death of his father. Cornell had a tough few years, more than most grown men could have handled without it breaking them."

The comment hit a nerve. She was opening her heart to Travis and he was using her words to find reasons for her son to become a criminal.

"We've talked enough," she said, her voice shaky. She walked to the kitchen area, found a glass and filled it with ice and water.

"I didn't mean to upset you, Faith."

"It doesn't matter, Travis. Nothing you say can change my mind about Cornell. He's a good kid. None of the hardships he went through changed that."

Tears came to her eyes and this time she didn't try to fight them back. She propped her elbows on the counter, buried her face in her hands and began to sob.

She heard Travis's footfalls and then felt his arms close around her. He held her tight until the sobs that racked her body grew still.

Then he tugged her around to face him. His thumb fitted under her chin and he nudged it up until she was staring into the depths of his dark eyes.

"I believe you, Faith. I don't see how anyone could have a mother like you and not be a loving, decent human. Now you have to believe me. I'll do everything in my power to help you find your son and clear his name."

"He's my world."

"I know."

In the same breath, Travis's lips found hers. She dissolved in the kiss, letting his heat and sweet reassurance wash over her and steal her breath away.

She didn't understand how passion could come in the midst of heartbreaking turmoil. All she knew was that it felt right to be in Travis's arms.

Finally, he pushed away. "I think we better stop," he said. "Unless…"

Unless she didn't want to. She didn't. She ached to fit herself in his arms and have him carry her to the bed. But would they both be sorry in the morning?

"I want you," she whispered. "But not tonight. Not until Cornell is safe and we have nothing between us but each other."

THE PAIN IN Cornell's side was growing worse. He'd pulled a muscle jumping across a fence and landing on a small ranch a few miles north of Laredo.

It was dark now, and there was light coming from just one room in the family home. Upstairs, a bedroom, he suspected. As long as he didn't do anything to upset the four horses in their stalls, he should be safe until morning.

Hunger pangs growled in his stomach. He'd drunk from the hose at the back of the barn, but he hadn't eaten since morning. He should have planned more thoroughly, but the idea had crystalized all at once. A plan to keep the artifacts out of Georgio's hands without openly double-crossing him.

Cornell had figured he could get away while they searched the horse trailer. He'd thought of it before, wondered if he'd have the nerve to make a run for it if he was caught in the act of smuggling. He'd seen others do so. Only once had he seen a man shot for trying to escape.

Cornell sat on a pile of hay and removed his boots— nice shoes, the kind a rancher's son would wear. That was what Georgio had said when he'd given them to him, along with the clothes he was to wear when he crossed the border with a shipment.

Just a few shipments. Not drugs. Not arms. Georgio had promised him that. Not that his promises meant much. He'd also promised that he'd set Cornell up with a job and a new identity on the West Coast.

The alternative was a prison cell for the rest of his

life or a cell on death row. At the time, it had seemed the only way out.

But Cornell was tired of living a lie. Sick at not being able to see anyone he cared about. Starting to hate himself for not standing up like a man and taking the punishment he deserved.

He was ready to turn himself in. The hardest part would be seeing the pain and heartbreak on his mother's face when he admitted the truth.

He had killed an unarmed man.

Chapter Thirteen

Travis spent another restless night, this one on a couch so short that his feet hung over the end. He could have pulled it out into a bed, but comfort was the least of his concerns.

A far bigger one was the fact that he could hear the sound of Faith's gentle breathing and imagine her lying between the sheets, her hair spread across the pillow, her soft breasts free.

The kiss had been his undoing. Any arguments he'd had for why he shouldn't fall for her were moot points now. He'd fallen and fallen hard.

He'd been with lots of other women. None had ever affected him the way Faith did. He couldn't explain it. Didn't understand it. Had no reference point for how love should make a man feel.

All he knew was that he would be there for her no matter what happened next, no matter what crime her son had or hadn't committed. Travis couldn't fathom not wanting to be with her every day for the rest of his life.

But if something happened to Cornell, would she ever be able to love anyone again?

When the first glow of dawn finally peeked around the edges of the drapes, he kicked off the sheet and padded to the kitchen to start a pot of coffee. He drank it in the morning quiet as he considered his next move.

Every law-enforcement agency in the state was looking for Cornell, especially now that they knew Georgio Trosclair might be the mastermind behind the smuggling. Georgio's sins were legend. He'd been getting away with drug trafficking and murder for years. There wasn't a cop worth the badge he wore who didn't want to have a hand in getting Georgio off the street and behind bars.

The bedroom door creaked just as Travis was about to start a fresh pot of coffee. He looked up. Faith stood in the doorway, her long brown hair rumpled from sleep, her face makeup-free, her eyes wide and haunted.

Desire hit so hard and fast he grew dizzy. But this was no time for weakness. He managed to pull it together.

"Good morning."

"What time is it?" she asked.

"Almost seven."

"I'm sorry. I never dreamed I'd sleep so late, but I was awake until after two."

"Then you needed the rest."

He flipped the switch on the coffeemaker. His cell phone rang. He grabbed it from the lamp table near the sofa and checked the caller ID. Reno.

"It's my partner," Travis said. He hated to talk in front of Faith in case it was bad news. "I'll be right outside."

He answered the phone as he closed the door behind him. "What's up?"

"Price of gas and a trace on the number that Angela Pointer used to call Faith."

"Good work. What's the location of origin?"

"About twenty miles north of Laredo. Phone is registered to Dolores Guiterrez."

"Any info on her?"

"She's married, has five kids, works as a cook at the Jackrabbit Chase Ranch."

"So I can probably find her there?"

"If not, I have an address for her, but here's the interesting part. Several calls were also made yesterday not from Dolores's cell phone but from Jackrabbit Chase Ranch to Georgio's encrypted cell phone, the first within a half hour after the contraband was confiscated."

"Suggesting the rancher might be the fence who was waiting for delivery."

"That's my take on it," Reno agreed. "So it's anyone's guess how Angela Pointer fits into this."

"Do we have a name for the rancher?"

"Alex Salinger, age sixty-three, well known in the community as an upright man—at least that's what I deducted from what I could find on him. He's connected to Georgio, so I'm sure there's more to the story."

"No doubt."

"All of this is out of our jurisdiction," Reno said, "so don't even think about going to the ranch."

"Is that your official position?"

"Yep. That said, give me a few hours and I'll be in Laredo to go there with you. We can't question Alex about the smuggling, but we can damn sure pretend to be looking for an old friend named Angela Pointer."

"Thanks for the offer, but you know I don't have a few hours. It's a race now to see who finds Cornell Ashburn first—law enforcement or one of Georgio's hit men."

"Either way, the kid is screwed," Reno said.

"But one way, he lives to tell about it."

"I'M NOT STAYING with some Department of Public Safety babysitter, Travis. I'm the one Angela called. She's a lot more likely to talk to me than to you."

"We don't even know that we'll find her there."

"I'm going with you."

"It could be dangerous."

"You'll protect me. And we don't have time to sit around arguing about protocol. I'll be showered and ready to go in ten minutes."

Travis threw up his hands in frustration. "Once we get to the ranch, you do exactly as I say. No wandering off by yourself and no taking over the conversation. I call the shots."

"I wouldn't want it any other way."

Faith let her hands drop from her hips, knowing she'd won. She had to talk to Angela. If she looked her in the eye, she'd know if the woman was lying.

And on the off chance that Angela really did have feelings for Cornell, surely she'd do everything she could to help Faith find Cornell. It wasn't just the best opportunity they had of finding her son quickly; it was the only option.

Travis pulled up to the gate at Jackrabbit Chase at exactly 8:48 a.m. The time was displayed on a digitalized keypad. This was a much more sophisticated operation than he'd anticipated.

The metal gate was locked and required a code to open it. He punched the call button, sporting a friendly smile for the surveillance camera as he did.

"Can I help you?" The voice was male, a bit gruff and scratchy.

"Sure hope so. If not, this is another of my wife's wild-goose chases," he said, sticking to the lies they'd rehearsed on the drive out. "She's looking for a friend of hers named Angela Pointer. We heard she was living here at Jackrabbit Chase Ranch."

"You heard wrong."

"You sure? We got it on good authority she was here."

"Someone gave you a bum steer. But hold on a minute. I'll check with the boss and make sure I'm giving you the straight of it. Can I have your names?"

"Sure. Calvin and Eloise Hartford. Eloise and Angela go way back, all the way to sixth grade. If we don't find her here, we'll just have to visit every ranch in the area until we find her."

The silence lasted about two minutes before the voice came back online. "Mr. Salinger said he can spare a few minutes. Just follow the main road for a quarter of a mile and you'll see the house on the right."

"Sure do appreciate that."

The gate opened. So far, so good.

Faith shifted restlessly and rearranged the visor to block the glare from the sun. "She's here. I know it. But we'll never see her. They're all in this together. Cornell is only a pawn. Whatever he did wrong was against his will."

"Just remember the rules," Travis cautioned again. "I do the talking. And there will be no mention of Cornell. Not by us. John Patterson's team will have a warrant when they come out, and they can search the premises."

"And by that time, my son may be dead."

"TALK ABOUT THE LIVES of the rich, famous and corrupt," Faith said as they approached the house.

The place looked more like a plantation house than a South Texas dwelling. It was white and three stories, with a wide staircase that led to the main entrance on the second level. Giant white columns supported a covered veranda.

Tall flagpoles bearing Texas and U.S. flags flanked

the circular drive. Perfectly manicured plots of green shrubs and blooming plants ran across the front of the massive house.

Travis parked and he and Faith climbed the outdoor stairs to the heavy wooden door on the second floor, where a man met them.

"I'm Alex Salinger. Welcome to my ranch."

"Damn nice house," Travis said. "I had no idea raising cattle made this much money."

Alex chuckled and clapped him on the back. "It helps if you have a rich pappy."

Or crooked friends.

Alex led them into a huge room with two chunky leather sofas and a stone fireplace. It was a man's room, as rugged as Salinger looked with his weathered face, whiskered chin and an eagle tattoo on his left biceps.

"My security man tells me you're looking for a woman named Angela Pointer," he said.

"Yeah. My wife's on a quest to find the daughter of her best friend who died years ago. You know how it is when a woman gets something in her mind. Can't be deterred."

"I sure wish I could help, but I've never heard of an Angela Pointer. Lots of people around here I've never heard of, though, so can't go by me. Have you tried the local sheriff?"

"That's next on our list," Travis said. "Do you have anyone working for you who might know her?"

"Not likely, but I'll ask around. Tell you what," Alex said, as if what he was about to say was an afterthought. "I'll have my cook bring you some coffee and you can ask her about your friend's daughter. Dolores knows everybody around these parts."

Dolores. That sealed the deal as far as Travis was concerned. Angela had called from the ranch using Dolores Guiterrez's phone, most likely at Alex's direction. He was fishing to find out if Travis and Faith knew where Cornell was hiding.

He knew the police would trace the call but he had no qualms about letting them talk to his cook because Dolores and everyone else who worked for him knew to keep their mouths shut.

Even if Travis searched the premises, there would be no sign of Angela. Alex Salinger, like Georgio, wouldn't make mistakes.

Only they had made one. Cornell had gotten caught smuggling their stolen goods.

Alex left and returned a minute later. He settled in an oversize dark brown recliner and propped a foot over his knee as if they were there for a friendly chat.

"Ever worked as a wrangler?" the rancher asked.

"Naw. I'm a mud logger. Started out as a worm years ago out in West Texas and moved up the ladder." Travis threw out the oil-field terms most Texans were familiar with.

"Really? You wear a Stetson and boots like the real McCoy."

Dolores appeared a minute later with a tray of filled coffee mugs and a platter of warm cinnamon buns that smelled too tempting to refuse. Travis took one of each.

Faith took a cup of coffee from the tray. It tipped in her hand and drops of the hot beverage spilled over the rim and into her lap.

She yelped and jumped up, brushing coffee from her pale gray slacks. Travis hurried to her aid, but Dolores got to her first. The woman started wiping at the spill with her apron.

"I'm so sorry," she said. "I shouldn't have filled the cups so full."

"It's okay," Faith assured her. "And it was my fault, not yours. I could use a wet cloth to wipe it off, though, before it stains."

"Of course."

Dolores hurried away, with Faith a step behind her. Travis realized almost immediately what was going on. Faith had spilled the coffee deliberately for a chance to talk to the woman in private.

So much for her promise to let him handle this. He started to go after her, but on second thought changed his mind. If anyone could get information out of Dolores, it was probably Faith. Woman to woman.

Faith returned a minute later, wet cloth in hand. Dolores wasn't with her.

Alex's phone rang. He excused himself to take the call. When he returned, he was clearly irritated. "I'd like to stay and talk, but I have to get back to work. I'll see you to the door."

Just as well, Travis thought. They were wasting their time here, though he'd love to know if the phone call Alex had received concerned Cornell.

The only way to prove Salinger was lying about Angela's having been there was for the local-law enforcement team to get a search warrant, and right now Angela was not their first priority.

Thankfully, apprehending Cornell was. But it had been hours since he'd disappeared. He could be hiding out in Mexico by now.

Or lying dead in a ditch or floating in the Rio Grande, the work of Georgio's hit men.

And that would tear the heart out of the woman Travis loved.

FURY BURNED INSIDE FAITH. Dolores was a mother. She of all people should have empathized with her. And she might have if she hadn't been so scared she'd turned a ghostly shade of white.

"Dolores didn't lie when I questioned her in the kitchen," Faith said, continuing the rant she'd started the second they'd left the ranch. "She was too scared to open her mouth. She just kept shaking her head and looking over her shoulder, as if she expected Alex to walk in on us. How can someone hold that much power over another individual in this day and age?"

"It happens more than you'd guess. From school-yard bullying to adult threats of intimidation. Some people thrive on control."

"Psychos without a conscience."

"Even if we'd located Angela and you'd been able to talk to her, I don't think she could have told you where to find Cornell."

"But you don't know that."

"No, but if Georgio and Salinger knew where to find Cornell, the phone call to you would have been pointless."

"So you think Dolores was charged with finding out if I'd talked to Cornell?"

"That's a definite possibility."

"I wish Cornell would call. If I could just hear his voice…"

"My guess is he doesn't want to drag you into this."

"Or maybe he fears my phone is bugged. Can we be sure it's not?"

"Yep."

"How?"

"It's being monitored. Any attempt to bug it will automatically send a signal to the precinct and to me and Reno."

"I never knew you could do that."

"Marvels of modern technology. The trick is staying one step ahead of the criminals."

"And we're not."

"Not yet," Travis said. "We have an all-points bulletin out for Cornell's arrest. He could be apprehended at any time. So just trust your gut feelings. You've said time and time again that once we find him, there will be an explanation for all of this."

"I'm sure of it." She had to hold on to that conviction with all the strength she had left.

"We need fuel," Travis said. "And I could use some breakfast. One cinnamon roll doesn't cut it for me."

"Fine," she said. "Stop anywhere. Toast and coffee are all I can handle."

Five minutes later, Travis pulled into a service station. Faith got out of the car to go to the restroom. She stretched, then stopped and looked around to see where the annoying knocking sound was coming from.

Instead of pumping gas, Travis was standing at the back of the car.

She hurried to join him. "What is that?"

"Step away, Faith." His tone was tense. His right hand was inside his lightweight wind jacket, no doubt resting on the butt of the small pistol he carried in a shoulder holster.

Her already edgy nerves reacted with a new wave of apprehension. The knocking sounded again—three taps, as if something were signaling them.

"Step away," he repeated.

This time she did as he said.

He looked around as if to make sure no one was standing too near before pushing the trunk release button on the car key.

The trunk opened slowly. The knocking stopped, replaced by a soft cry, similar to the mew of an injured cat. Two bare feet and one thin arm poked out.

"What the hell?" Travis reached in and offered a hand to the young woman who emerged. She tried to stand, but winced in pain and leaned against the back fender for support.

"Who are you and how did you get in my trunk?" Travis asked.

She looked around nervously and then turned to Faith. "I'm Angela Pointer. We talked last night and also a few nights before, when I warned you to stay away from Georgio."

"Both phone calls were from you?"

She nodded."

The young woman was nothing like the seductive, heartless cougar Faith had pictured. She was pretty but incredibly thin and probably not much over Cornell's age. Her hair was dishwater blond, straight and long. Her eyes revealed a troubled innocence that touched Faith in spite of the circumstances.

"Who locked you in the trunk?" Faith asked.

"No one. Sending me with you is the last thing Alex Salinger would do. He'd have killed me before he'd let me talk to you. He locked me in an upstairs bedroom and ordered me to keep quiet after his bodyguard announced you were at the ranch gate."

Faith exhaled slowly as the new and ever-changing reality sank in. "So Alex knew who we were all along."

"He's known who you were ever since you first showed up at the Passion Pitt," Angela said. "And Georgio made sure he knew who Detective Dalton is."

"How did you get out of a locked room?" Travis asked, his voice tinged with suspicion.

"I climbed out the window, crawled over the veranda railing and dropped to the ground." She reached down and massaged her swollen ankle. "That's how I got hurt."

"You could have gotten a lot more than a sprained or broken ankle," Travis said.

"And if I hadn't escaped, I would have been killed—not today, but eventually. I know too much for them to let me live. Besides, they have no reason to keep me around now that they don't need me to help keep Cornell in line."

"I don't understand," Faith said.

"I'll explain everything, but not here. We're too close to the ranch, and Alex and his so-called security staff are no doubt searching for me."

"I have enough fuel to get us a few miles farther and off the main highway," Travis said. "I'll help you into the backseat. But before we do anything, I need you to answer one question for me. Not lies. Not games."

"If I can," Angela said.

"Do you know where we can find Cornell?"

"No. All I know is what he told me when he called, just before dumping his phone into the Rio Grande."

"Which was?"

"He's on the run from Georgio and the law. He just wants to stay alive."

"How did he contact you?"

"Through Dolores Guiterrez. She's a good woman, but she's scared of Alex. Really scared. We all are."

"Okay," Travis said. "But I'd best not find out you're lying to me. If I do, I can promise you a jail cell."

"I'm through with the lies," Angela said.

"Then we'll talk. After that, you need to see a doctor about that ankle. It might be broken."

"No doctors," she declared. "No hospitals. Not in Laredo. It's too risky."

"We can argue medical care later," Faith said. "Let's just get out of here." The young woman's fear was contagious and Faith was desperate to hear what she had to say about Cornell before Alex showed up and chaos ensued.

But first she needed the answer to one important question of her own. Faith waited until they were in the car and the engine was running.

"Where's the baby, Angela? Where's my grandchild?"

Chapter Fourteen

Angela leaned forward, her gaze locked with Faith's. "How did you know about that?"

"The same way I heard that my son was involved with you—from a forensic analysis of his computer. Were you pregnant?"

"I was, but I miscarried in the first trimester. The baby wasn't Cornell's. My ex-boyfriend convinced me to give our relationship one last chance. It was a mistake. I knew that within the week, but though I wasn't aware of the fact, I was pregnant when I called everything off again.

"I know it's hard for you to believe, considering all the trouble I brought on your family, but I never had sex with your son."

That twisted the situation even more. If there was nothing between Angela and Cornell but a crush on his part, it was incredible that this had gone so far astray.

"Are you denying that you encouraged Cornell to leave home and run away with you?"

"I begged him to stay away from me and the Passion Pit. He didn't listen."

"Because he was so infatuated with you."

"No, because he has a heart of gold and he wouldn't walk away when he knew I was in trouble."

"I saw the notes he wrote you, Angela. He fancied himself in love with you."

"I'm not denying there was a strong attraction between us. I've never known anyone as honest and giving as your son. But I didn't fool myself. I've always known he deserved better than me."

Honest. Giving. A heart of gold. Those were all the things Faith knew to be true about Cornell. And yet... "All I know is that one day I had a son who was happy, who came home every night. A son who confided in me and laughed with me. Then he met you and vanished into thin air. Now there's a warrant out for his arrest."

"I know. His life is ruined."

"How did it happen? I have to know, Angela. What made Cornell turn to a man like Georgio?"

The young woman started to cry softly. Faith felt sorry for her. She truly did. But Angela was here and safe, at least for now. Cornell was on the run from the law and a man who'd see him dead before he'd let him confess his crimes.

"I think we should table this conversation until we get back to the motel," Travis urged. "And then we need to discuss it as calmly as possible—without accusations and recriminations. There will be plenty of time for those later."

"I can't go to a motel with you." Panic bled into Angela's voice. "That's the first place Alex and his men will look for me."

"I can't dump you on the street," Travis said. "Either you trust me to protect you or we go directly to the police, and you can tell your story to them. You might be able to persuade them to put you in protective custody. It's your decision."

"I can't go to the police. If I tell the truth, it will harm Cornell. I'd rather be dead than cause him more trouble."

"Then I guess you're stuck with me for a while."

Travis stopped for fuel and then at a fast-food chain with a drive-through lane. He ordered breakfast sandwiches and coffee for all of them. He also got a cup of ice for Angela to hold against her swollen ankle.

Faith tried to eat, but one bite into the sandwich she grew nauseated. Angela had promised to explain everything, but in the end it would just be more talk. She couldn't tell them where to find Cornell, and nothing else mattered at this point.

Faith reached into her pocket and touched her phone, willing it to ring. If she could only hear from Cornell, they could go to him. He surely knew that no matter what he'd done, she would never turn her back on him.

She closed her eyes and then opened them quickly as a deadly premonition wrapped strangling fingers around her heart. She might never see her son again.

As if reading her pain, Travis reached for her hand and squeezed it.

But even Detective Travis Dalton, as amazing as he was, couldn't win all the time.

By the time they reached the motel, Angela's ankle was turning a weird shade of purple. Travis picked her up and carried her inside. They used a side door that opened into a courtyard to avoid questions from the attendant at the front desk.

Unfortunately, the cleaning lady was just finishing with their suite. She moved out of the way as Travis situated Angela on the sofa and Faith retrieved pillows from the bedroom to elevate her leg.

"What happened? Did you fall?"

"It's just a sprain," Angela answered quickly. "I wasn't looking and twisted it stepping off the curb."

"I'll get you some ice."

"Thanks."

The cleaning lady rolled the vacuum cleaner out into the hall as she went for the ice.

"I NEED TO MAKE one quick call to Reno," Travis said. "I'd appreciate it if you save the explanations until I'm through. No use having to repeat everything for my benefit."

"We'll wait," Faith agreed.

An awkward silence filled the room when he stepped out. Now that the moment of truth had arrived, she wasn't sure she wanted to hear it.

If Angela's talking to the police would harm Cornell, then the facts might not set him free. Still, better a jail cell for a little while than living on the run.

"Any news?" Faith asked when Travis rejoined them.

"Nothing. Hopefully, you can shed some light on what's going on, Angela. How did Cornell get mixed up in a smuggling operation?"

She had the look of a prisoner facing a firing squad. Faith sucked in her breath and waited for an explanation that might destroy her world.

"I guess I should start at the beginning."

"Please do," Faith said. "Don't sugarcoat anything. I can't fight for Cornell unless I know exactly how he got into this situation."

Angela curled her long blond hair around her fingertips, twisting it first one way and then the other. Her eyes remained downcast, her long lashes shielding them from view.

"Cornell came into the Passion Pit one night with a bunch of his high-school friends."

"How did they get in if they were all underage?"

"They had fake IDs. All the teenagers carry them these days. Old enough to go to war at eighteen, old enough to drink and go to see a scantily clothed woman dance around a pole. That's how most of them see it."

"Is that the night you met him?"

"Yes. My ex-boyfriend showed up and started trouble. Georgio had warned him never to come inside the club when he was high, but there was no reasoning with him in that condition."

"What kind of trouble?" Faith asked.

"He cornered me as I was leaving the stage to work the tables. I tried to fight him off, but he was touching me, you know, sliding his hand inside my G-string and trying to kiss my nipples, that sort of thing."

Faith's stomach rolled as the image seared into her brain.

"Where was the bouncer?" Travis asked.

"Dealing with a rowdy customer. Before he realized what was going on and could get to me, Cornell caught Walt off guard. He threw a punch that sent Walt's head slamming into the wall.

"Blood poured from his nose, and his eyes rolled back into his head. He literally passed out for a few seconds. When he came to, he pulled himself to his feet and staggered toward Cornell, fists up for a fight.

"The men in the room started yelling to Cornell to finish him off. Fortunately, the bouncer reached them before another punch was thrown.

"He would have tossed them both out, but I intervened. I was scared that if they left together the fight would continue on the street and Cornell would get roughed up bad.

Walt was crazy when he was high, and a street fighter. Knives, blades, broken beer bottles, metal pipes. He was skilled in all of them."

Angela's voice grew shaky. She stopped talking, but finally looked up and faced Faith. "If Cornell would have left with his friends, it would have all been over. They'd have had a laugh over the fight and then forgotten about it."

Faith shared Angela's regrets. But all the ifs in the world wouldn't change things now. "What did happen?"

"I had a drink with Cornell. We connected. I'd never met anyone like Cornell. He didn't come on to me sexually or start bragging about what a big shot he was. We just talked, like old friends."

"He was a very special kid," Faith murmured.

"Almost a man," Angela reminded her. "He came back to the club a couple of times that week. On each occasion we had a chance to talk. It was two weeks before he kissed me. From that moment on our relationship changed."

That, Faith could identify with. But Cornell was so young. As she had been when she'd hooked up with Cornell's father. But the relationship had given her Cornell, and she would never be sorry for that.

"Cornell didn't want to lie to you, Mrs. Ashburn. He loves you very much. After he kissed me, he wanted me to come home with him and meet you."

"Why didn't you?"

"I knew you wouldn't be blinded like Cornell. You'd see right through me and realize how wrong I was for him."

"Yet you didn't break up with him?"

"I couldn't. He made me feel decent and special. He saw me as more than an exotic dancer. When he found out I was pregnant, he begged me to leave my job and let him take care of me. He wanted to quit school and get a job. For a few days, even I got wrapped up in the fantasy."

"He wanted to take care of you even though you were pregnant with another man's child?"

"He did. How could I not love him for that?" Angela moved her ankle and rearranged the hand towel and ice, wincing as she did so.

"Is that when Cornell went to work for Georgio?" Travis asked.

"No. Cornell would never have willingly had anything to do with Georgio. He hadn't even met him at that point, though evidently Georgio knew about us. I'm sure Walt told him."

The story seemed to be going in circles. Faith was no closer to understanding how a teenage infatuation had led Cornell into smuggling stolen religious artifacts across the border. "So your ex-boyfriend and Georgio were friends," she said in an effort to keep the order of events straight.

"Walt worked for him."

"Doing what?" Travis asked.

"Keeping the customers happy. He sold them crack cocaine, marijuana, ecstasy—anything they wanted, except when the narcs were around. Sniffing out narcs was Walt's specialty."

"I still don't understand," Faith said. "If Cornell didn't go to work for Georgio, how did he become a smuggler?"

"Walt decided he wanted me back. Apparently, he started a fight with Cornell one night when I was in the backstage dressing room. The bouncer threw them out. That's when I heard the shots."

Travis leaned forward. "Gunshots?"

Angela nodded. "I ran out of the dressing room and into the bouncer, who had come after me."

"Does this bouncer have a name?"

"Brad. That's all I ever heard him called. Anyway, he said Georgio wanted to see me. When I got to his office, Cornell was sitting in a chair, the front of his shirt covered in blood. I thought he was the one who'd been shot. I ran to him, but he pushed me away. He wouldn't look at me. Wouldn't talk to me."

The dread swelled in Faith's chest until every beat of her heart felt as if it were knocking against cement. She listened, stunned, as Angela told how Georgio had found Cornell standing over Walt's dead body, the murder weapon in Cornell's hand.

He'd shot Walt in the back of the head. He'd killed in cold blood an unarmed man walking away from him.

"No. Cornell would never do that. He couldn't." For a second Faith didn't even realize that her anguished cries had come from her lips instead of just echoing through her entire being.

Travis pulled her to her feet and into his arms. He held her against him, so close she could feel his own heart beating against her chest.

When she finally stopped shaking, she pulled away. "Finish what you have to say, Angela." She'd hear the words, but she would never believe her boy was a murderer.

"Cornell didn't deny that he'd killed Walt. He was ready to call the cops and confess. Georgio convinced him that he shouldn't."

"Did he also convince him not to call me?" Faith asked. "I'm his mother. I should have been with him, helping him make the decisions that would follow him forever."

"Cornell didn't want to hurt you, Mrs. Ashburn. He was worried more about you than he was about himself."

Worried, but he'd shut her out. He still was shutting her out. Somehow she'd failed him. A mother's love hadn't been enough.

The rest of the explanation began to blur in Faith's mind. Georgio had offered Cornell a way out. He'd make sure no one connected him to a crime that might send him to the electric chair. All Cornell had to do was go into hiding until the investigation blew over.

Georgio had insisted Angela leave town as well, since the cops would surely question her about the murder. That way she wouldn't have to lie to them.

Angela had encouraged Cornell to accept Georgio's offer. She'd gone to the Jackrabbit Chase Ranch and lived in isolation, warned that the cops were looking for her and that she had to lie low. Cornell had gone to live with one of Georgio's contacts living in Mexico, an American named Tom.

She'd talked to Cornell only on rare occasions after that. At first he'd told her that he was transporting horses across the border. It wasn't until a couple weeks ago, when she'd overheard a conversation between Alex and Georgio, that she realized Cornell was smuggling contraband. That was when she'd become a prisoner instead of a guest.

"Alex had me call you a few nights ago. He made me tell you to stop searching for Cornell."

"You also said to stay away from Georgio."

"That was only to throw you off. You must hate me for the role I played in this," Angela said.

"I'm not sure how I feel about you," Faith said.

"I understand and I don't blame you if you hate me. Just drive me to the border. I'll get out of your life forever."

But it was too late for that now. The damage was done. "No. You're coming back to Dallas with us," Faith said. "The lies, the blackmail, the fear—it has to end. Besides, you've already confessed everything to the best homicide detective in Dallas. There's no point in running."

A homicide detective who'd be instrumental in sending her son to prison for the rest of his life, if not the electric chair.

If she'd had any hope of a future with Travis, it had just come to an end, along with all her dreams for Cornell's future.

"If I go back to Dallas, Georgio will track me down and have me killed," Angela said. "Maybe that's what I deserve."

"It's Georgio and Alex who need to get what they deserve," Travis said. "I plan to make sure they do. In the meantime, I'll get you full-time police protection."

"Where will I live? I have no money. No job. No friends I can trust."

"You'll live at the Dry Gulch Ranch with Faith and me for now. R.J. wants family, and he's about to get some, with all the complications that go with it. That won't begin to make up for the pain and suffering he put me through when he left me to be raised by foster parents who hated and abused me."

"I'm not family," Angela said.

"Nor am I," Faith added.

"That's okay. He'll like you both better than he ever liked me," Travis said.

CORNELL JERKED AWAKE. Something furry was inside his pants, climbing up his thigh. He unzipped his jeans and shimmied out of them. The tarantula skimming his briefs was unperturbed.

He knocked the big creature away and leaned against the trunk of the tree he'd been sleeping under, trying to catch his breath and get his bearings.

The dregs of sleep disappeared and reality set in again. It was far more frightening than dealing with the wicked-looking spider.

The air was chilly. He'd lost his jacket, probably left it back at that horse barn he'd tried to sleep in last night.

He remembered sneaking out of the building before daylight when one of the mares began to neigh and stamp, protesting the nearness of the stranger who'd invaded her space. With only moonlight to illuminate his path, he'd stumbled upon a fence line and then followed the strings of barbwire until he'd reached the creek, where he'd stopped to rest and evidently fallen asleep.

He reached for his phone to check the time, then remembered he'd hurled it into the Rio Grande after making that last call to Dolores. He'd wanted Angela and his mother to know he was safe.

Safe. Georgio had promised him that once. What a joke. A man nobody crossed unless he had a suicide wish, though Cornell hadn't figured that out until long after he'd sold his soul to the devil.

Now he had crossed the devil. Georgio wouldn't know at first that it was Cornell who'd tipped off the border patrol that the horse trailer would be carrying more than steeds. But it wouldn't matter.

He had screwed up. Georgio had no patience for people who screwed up, especially when they knew as much about his business as Cornell did.

But Cornell didn't care anymore. They'd made a prisoner of Angela. Even if Cornell had continued to play by the rules, it was only a matter of time until Georgio came to the conclusion that he and Angela were dispensable.

It was past time for someone to take the monster down. All Cornell had to do was get to the police and tell all before Georgio found and killed him. Then both of them could rot in prison. A man should pay for his crimes.

Cornell pulled on his jeans and started walking again. By the time he reached a country road, the sun indicated it was midmorning. He walked along the shoulder, stopping to put up a thumb when a car passed.

He figured he'd walked a good two miles before someone finally slowed down. A black sedan with a man in the passenger seat.

"Need a lift?"

"If you're going into Laredo."

"Sure. Get in."

Cornell took one step toward the car before he saw the gun. He started to run. Shots cracked through the still air. Blood splattered the ground around him like red rain.

He pushed on, staggering toward the fence. He grabbed for a fence post. He missed and the earth rose to meet him. The world went black.

But he could hear his mother's voice calling to him, pleading with him to come home.

"I love you, Mother. I'm so sorry I let you down."

Chapter Fifteen

"Sounds awful fishy to me," Reno said. "Did Cornell even own a gun?"

"Not according to Faith. And I don't remember a body showing up outside the Passion Pit ten months ago."

"Had there been, we would definitely have remembered, since we were already knocking ourselves out trying to find some solid evidence against Georgio."

"We had evidence," Travis corrected. "An eyewitness who conveniently fell from a ladder and died before he could testify."

"And now we have Cornell, who could possibly testify that Georgio had him kill Walt, except that his testimony would also send Cornell to prison, so why confess? Georgio always manages to stay ahead of the game."

"Only why would Cornell go along with that?" Travis questioned. "Supposedly, he wasn't an addict, so that counts out his doing it to get drugs. He had no police record, no juvenile infractions. No history of violence of any kind. I checked his school records just before I called you. He was never even suspended for fighting."

"There's always a first time, and women can bring out the worst in a guy."

"So I've heard."

"But then we have Walt Marshall," Reno continued.

"I also talked with his high-school counselor. He was expelled in the eleventh grade for bringing a gun to school. Before that he had a number of suspensions for fighting, including one for threatening a teacher."

"Have you talked to that teacher?"

"No, but I left a message for her to call me once she's out of class for the day. In the meantime, I'll check out the national database and see what kind of rap sheet he's accumulated."

"And see if he ever showed up in the Dallas morgue," Travis said. "But for now, the first order of business is making sure Cornell stays alive."

"I guess that means no arrests have been made yet."

"Not that I've heard," Travis said grimly. "I have a call in to Patterson so I can fill him in on Angela's story and see if there's been any progress in locating Cornell. John should be calling me back any minute."

"How's Faith taking this?"

"She's hanging in there, still holding out hope that this is all some huge mistake."

"Ever met a mother who didn't think her son was innocent?"

"Only one. Gloria Keating. Called 911 and reported he'd stolen her heroin."

Reno laughed. "I remember. She was a jewel of a mom."

The difference was that Faith was a loving mother and this was pure agony for her. Before meeting Faith, Travis had been obsessed with putting Georgio behind bars. He still wanted that, but it was killing him that accomplishing that goal might send Faith's son to prison, as well.

For the first time in his life, he wished he wasn't a cop.

His phone clicked. "I've got another call, probably

Patterson. I need to talk to him while he's available, but phone me once you get the lowdown on Walt."

"I'm on it," Reno said. "I'll keep you posted and you do the same."

Travis switched the call to John. "Any news?"

"Yeah. Is Faith Ashburn still with you?"

"Yep. A few feet away, but out of hearing."

"Then I hope you're good at delivering devastating news."

Travis's muscles tensed. He swallowed a curse, afraid to even speculate about what was coming next.

"Cornell was found by a rancher out checking his fence line for breaks about an hour ago," Patterson said. "He was covered in blood and lying facedown in the grass. The rancher took him for dead at first, but then found a weak pulse and called for an ambulance."

"Gunshot wounds?"

"Two of them. Shot at close range, once in the shoulder, once in the back of the head. Whoever shot him probably believed they'd killed him, or they would have finished him off."

"The shooter will have holy hell to pay when Georgio finds out Cornell isn't dead."

"I hope Cornell rallies enough to talk before he dies," Patterson said.

"Any idea where Salinger was at the time of the shooting?" Travis asked.

"Sitting on the deck of his ranch house, drinking coffee and talking to me. I paid a friendly visit to Jackrabbit Chase this morning."

"Did he admit to you that Angela Pointer had been living on his ranch for the past ten months?"

"To the contrary, he swore he'd never heard of her. His word against Angela's. Take that to a jury and guess who they'll believe? The generous, well-respected rancher or the Big D stripper?"

"I picked her up at his ranch," Travis reminded him.

"No, you found her in your trunk at a gas station. A good defense attorney will twist that every which way but straight."

That still left Dolores Guiterrez, but Travis knew she'd be too afraid to testify against Salinger. Even if she risked it, she'd never live to take the stand. She'd have some kind of freak accident.

A fall. An accidental drowning. A house fire. Georgio's methods were effective if not particularly creative.

Here they went again.

"Exactly where is the ranch where Cornell was found?"

"About twenty-five miles north of here. Reports from the scene of the crime indicate the shooting took place just off the narrow shoulder of a little-used county road. He apparently stayed conscious long enough to stagger into a clump of tall grass along the fence line."

"Where is he now?"

"Doctor's Hospital, in surgery. His condition is listed as critical."

"Georgio didn't waste any time."

"No," John agreed. "Pisses me off that his thugs were more effective at finding him than we were, but it is what it is."

"They had to get tipped off from somebody," Travis said. "I'm sure Salinger has his own web of informants in these parts." But right now, Travis could think only about Faith and how she'd take the news. "Can Cornell's mom see him?"

"As far as I'm concerned, as long as the surgeon doesn't object. The kid is under arrest and there's a guard stationed at the door, but I'll see that the two of you are allowed in to see him."

"I appreciate that. I'll need someone to stay with Angela Pointer. She's scared to death that Salinger is going to track her down and kill her."

"Drop her off here. It's safe enough. But no questioning Cornell about the smuggling, Travis. I don't want anything to come back and bite me when this case goes to trial."

"No questions," he agreed. The smuggling charge was the least of Travis's concerns now. It was the murder charge that worried him.

That and the fact that there would be no way he could protect Faith from this new bombshell.

Travis thanked John for keeping him on the inside track and broke the connection.

Now came the hard part.

FAITH'S EYES OVERFLOWED with tears as she stepped into the intensive-care unit and got her first look at her wounded son. His eyes were closed. His skin ghostly pale. His breathing erratic in spite of the numerous tubes attached to his body. The monitors measuring his vital signs clicked ominously in the background.

She reached over and caressed his hand with her fingers and then brushed her lips across his cheek. "I'm here, Cornell," she whispered. "I'm here beside you. You're safe."

He didn't open his eyes or twitch or show any sign that he knew she was there.

She turned to the nurse, who was only steps away. "Can he hear me?"

"I'm not sure, but it never hurts to reassure him. He

may recognize your voice and get comfort from that even though he's not conscious."

"Has he regained consciousness at all since the shooting?"

"Not since arriving at the hospital, but the doctors don't want him to just yet. He's being kept in a medically induced semi-coma to avoid unwanted stress. It's not uncommon to do that after a traumatic brain injury."

A traumatic brain injury. The words conjured up new horrifying possibilities. She grabbed hold of the bed rail to support her watery muscles. "How serious is the injury?"

"I think it's best to discuss that with the surgeon. We've alerted him that you're here and he said he'll see you momentarily."

She couldn't blame the nurse for not wanting to be the bearer of bad news. Faith finally had her son back, but the nightmare had acquired new monsters.

Painful memories returned in a rush of sickening anxiety. She'd been through this before during the worst of the virus. Sat at Cornell's bedside, praying, crying, afraid to close her eyes for fear he wouldn't be alive when she opened them again.

How could life do this to Cornell and to her all over again?

She took a deep breath when she felt Travis's hand on her arm. Amazingly, his strength seemed to transfuse from his veins to hers. Sometime over the past few days he'd changed from cop to protector.

She didn't fully understand their new relationship, but he was the one person in the world she wanted with her right now. The one person she could lean on.

The feeling of being protected was only an illusion.

Travis was a cop. He would come down on the side of the law no matter what that meant for Cornell.

Even knowing that, she needed his touch. She let her head fall to his shoulder. He raked a hand through her hair, smoothing it and brushing it back from her cheeks.

"Thanks for being here," she whispered.

"I'll be here as long as you let me, Faith."

The doctor walked into the room. He introduced himself, then checked out his patient and the chart before turning back to Faith.

"I'm sure you have lots of questions," he said. "There's a small conference space off the waiting room where we can have some privacy."

They followed him past the guard and out of ICU.

"I realize my patient is under arrest," the doctor said once they'd reached the conference room. "Let me assure you, Mrs. Ashburn, that will not affect my treatment. Nor will it keep me from being as honest with you as possible."

"Thank you."

"There's no necessity for you to have Detective Dalton in the room with us now unless you want him here."

"He's also a friend. I'd like him to stay."

"Very well." The surgeon motioned for her and Travis to take a seat at the small round table, and he sat down, as well.

"How serious are the injuries?" she asked.

"Critical."

The doctor pulled two X-rays from Cornell's chart and showed her where the bullets had entered his body. He followed that with a string of medical jargon that was difficult to follow.

Faith studied the X-rays and then pushed them back

across the table. "Exactly what does that mean in layman's terms?"

"We removed the bullet from the shoulder, and barring any complications from infection, there should be no lasting impairment of the muscles."

"And the bullet to the head?"

"Brain injuries are never totally predictable, but I was able to remove the bullet without any further damage and stop the bleeding. There is temporary swelling that's pressing against the skull and extensive trauma to the tissue at the entry point.

"However, your son was extremely lucky, Mrs. Ashburn. If the bullet had hit an inch to the right or at a more direct angle, I doubt Cornell would be alive right now."

Faith trembled, hearing how close her son had come to death. But he was alive. God had been with him this morning, the same way He'd been with him during his illness.

"What are his chances for a complete recovery?" she asked.

"Right now I'd say good, assuming he makes it through the next twenty-four hours. This is the most critical period for him. But recovery will take time and most likely require rehabilitation."

"How much time?"

"That's impossible to predict. He could be fully functioning in as little as a few months or he might never regain all his facilities for memory and movement. Right now I think the former is more likely, but I can't promise that."

The odds were in his favor. That was enough for now. Only what chance for recovery would he have in prison?

"I'd like to stay with him tonight," Faith murmured.

"I understand," the doctor said. "I'll see that you're allowed to. But that brings up our next concern."

"Which is?"

"If all goes well tonight, I'd like to transfer your son to a trauma unit in Dallas either tomorrow or the following day. It's one of the best facilities in the country for this type of injury."

Faith considered the tubes and monitors he was hooked up to. She'd love to have him in Dallas, but... "Do you think it's wise to move him so soon?"

"Not by ambulance, but we'll arrange for an emergency medical air transport. A trauma nurse will travel with him. Do you have any problems with that?"

"Not if you're sure it's safe."

"I wouldn't recommend it if I wasn't convinced it was not only safe but a sound medical intervention for Cornell."

Back to Dallas, as soon as tomorrow. They would be going home. But that also meant they'd be closer to Georgio Trosclair, the monster who'd ruined Cornell's life and surely had a role in trying to kill him.

"Will Cornell still have a guard at his door when he's moved to Dallas?"

"You'll have to discuss that with John Patterson."

"He'll have a guard," Travis assured her. "I guarantee you that neither Georgio nor any of his thugs will get near Cornell while he's in the hospital."

She breathed easier, determined to see the positive side of this. Cornell was not only alive, but was getting the best medical treatment available. And he'd be in Dallas, where she could see him every day. That was miracle enough for now.

As long as he made it through the night.

ANGELA, FAITH AND TRAVIS drove through the gate at the Dry Gulf Ranch at 4:30 p.m. two days later.

Fortunately, Cornell had come through the first night at the hospital in Laredo without any serious complications and had made steady progress since then. Faith had left his bedside only once, long enough to go back to the motel for a quick shower and change of clothes.

She was clearly exhausted. Even the surgeon had noticed. He'd urged her to stay home and get a good night's rest tonight while the Dallas trauma team completed their evaluation.

While she'd been at the hospital, Travis had spent his time at the local police department, using their resources to dig up every speck of information he could on Walt Marshall. There was plenty to be found.

Walt had a history of arrests for everything from possession, distribution and trafficking of controlled substances to road rage and assault with a deadly weapon.

He'd served three years in a Georgia prison for the last charge. Shortly after his release he'd moved to Dallas. No surprise that he and Georgio had found each other.

Travis spotted Leif's car as they drove up to the house, though Faith was so preoccupied with her own concerns she didn't appear to notice. Just as well; she could use a pleasant surprise.

"It's a big house," Angela said as she climbed from the backseat of Travis's double-cab truck, which they'd picked up at the Lamberts' after Tague had flown them home from Laredo. "Your father must get lonesome living in it all by himself."

My father. The expression always threw him. Planting his seed in Travis's mother did not make R.J. a father any more that sowing hayseed made a man a rancher.

"I still don't feel right about imposing all my problems on him," Faith said. "His brain tumor is more than enough for him to deal with."

Angela stopped in her tracks. "He has a brain tumor? You didn't mention that. Is he bedridden?"

"He still gets around," Faith said, "just not like he used to. He gets dizzy and confused occasionally, but most of the time he's lucid. He goes horseback riding down to his favorite fishing hole every day. At least that's what his new daughter-in-law, my friend Joni, told me."

"I love horses," Angela said. "I used to ride when my father was alive."

The front door opened before they reached it. Joni flew out and came running to meet them. The signs of fatigue vanished from Faith's face. Her smile was radiant. Travis had never been as grateful to anyone as he was to Joni at that moment.

The two friends collapsed into each other's arms and the tears started to flow down both their faces.

R.J. and Leif were waiting at the door.

Leif gave Travis a manly clap on the back, but then pulled him into a half hug. "Welcome back, bro. Tough week?"

"*Tough* is not the word I'd use for it," Travis said, "but you're on the right track."

"Mighty glad to have you back," R.J. said. "Who's the young woman?"

Travis introduced Angela as a friend of Cornell's. He'd save the details for later, when he had a chance to talk to Leif alone.

R.J. flashed a big grin for Angela and escorted her inside.

"I want to hear everything," Leif said. "Adam and

Hadley are bringing dinner down here around six, so we need to find some alone time before that."

"Good idea. R.J. can show Angela to a bedroom, and Faith and Joni won't even notice that we're not around."

Travis had no qualms about leveling with Leif. He'd give him the inside scoop on everything. Well, almost everything. He'd leave out the part about falling so hard for Faith that he couldn't think straight where she was concerned.

That didn't change the fact that he might have to be instrumental in sending her son to prison.

Talk about a dead-end relationship.

"Why don't you ladies take a break and we men will clean up the kitchen?" Adam suggested.

"I agree," Leif said. "But I may finish off that blackberry cobbler first. I don't normally like cobbler or blackberries, but that is one scrumptious dessert."

Hadley passed him the remaining cobbler. "It's Caroline Lambert's recipe. She taught me how to make the crust, too. That's the real secret to good cobbler."

"Caroline as in Tague's mother?" Travis asked.

"Yes, she's an amazing cook. In fact, she's pretty amazing at everything she does."

"I can't believe some man hasn't grabbed her up and married her," R.J. said. "'Course, old Hugh will be a hard man to replace."

"He must be," Hadley said. "Caroline speaks of him often. I'm sure she still misses him."

Faith stood and started clearing the dishes from diningroom table.

Adam took them from her. "Seriously, get out of the kitchen. The men have KP duty tonight."

Leif and Travis added their agreement.

"You don't have to tell me twice, lover boy." Hadley handed Adam an apron and kissed him on the cheek. "Besides, I'd best check on Angela and make sure Lacy and Lila haven't worn her out."

"It was thoughtful of her to take them outside to catch fireflies while we visited over dessert."

"I think the girls with their energy and giggles are just what Angela needs," Faith said.

"I'd love to hear her life story," Joni interjected, "but no rush. I know everything is still part of an ongoing investigation." She put her arm around Faith's waist. "I'm just glad you're both here on the ranch with friends and family. One of the things I've learned from my brilliant, marvelous husband is that everything is easier to face when you're with people who love you."

Faith wasn't actually family, but she had to admit she felt more at home here tonight than she had anywhere since Cornell's disappearance.

But then anywhere with Travis might feel like that.

R.J. STAYED AT the table nursing a cup of decaf coffee that had grown cold. He looked surprised when the men rejoined him, each with a cold beer in hand.

He pushed his cup away. "Where's Gwen?"

"Do you mean Mattie Mae or Hadley?" Adam asked.

"If I'd meant 'em I would have said 'em. What did you do with Gwen?"

It was the same name he'd asked about the night of the wedding reception, when Travis had found him disoriented and confused.

"Gwen don't like beer in the house. If she sees you guys with those beers, she's gonna throw you out."

"It's okay," Adam said, trying to calm him. "She's

probably already gone to bed. Why don't I walk you to your bedroom and then we'll throw out the beers?"

"You better. She gets so mad she's like a cranky mule. No reasoning with that woman."

"You got that right," Adam agreed. "Let her sleep. I'll take care of things in here." He helped R.J. from his chair and then led him out of the dining room.

"What's with all the Gwen stuff?" Travis asked when Adam returned.

"Time travel, we think. Gwen was the middle name of his first wife, though who knows if that's the Gwen he's looking for. His doctor said it's not unusual for a brain tumor patient to confuse the past with the present. It also happens with a lot of healthy elderly folks."

"Does he get confused like that often?"

"Usually once or twice a week, but it never lasts long. It usually occurs when he's excited or upset about something. He's been worried about you and Faith ever since you flew to Laredo."

"How much does he know about that?"

"Just what I told him on the phone yesterday," Leif said. "That you found her missing son and he's in the hospital. I didn't mention the shooting or the arrest, so he thinks Cornell is sick."

"I don't know much more than that," Adam admitted. "Not that it's any of my business."

"Actually, it is," Travis said. "Leif and I talked just before dinner, but I won't make any decisions about having Faith and Angela stay here unless you okay my plan. After all, this is your home. I'm the outsider."

"Then let's hear it."

"Better get another beer first," Travis said. "This gets complicated."

An hour later, they'd agreed on a plan that they could

all live with. Hadley and the girls would spend a few days with her mother, a visit they'd already been talking about.

Joni would have the option of staying with the Lamberts for a few days or at the big house anytime she was at the ranch when Leif wasn't around. That wouldn't be often, since most of the day she was making her rounds as a large-animal vet.

Angela, Faith and R.J. would have two police officers on duty at the ranch house anytime Travis couldn't be there to protect them. That way, if any of them left the house to go horseback riding or just to get outdoors for a walk, they could have an armed bodyguard with them.

"How do you think R.J. will react to having guards around?" Travis asked.

"I'll tell him they're some of your cop friends, just here on vacation to do some riding and get in some target practice," Leif said.

Adam nodded. "R.J. will buy that and talk their ears off. I'm a former marine, you know. Getting in some target practice of my own against a man like Georgio would be downright fun. But do you really think he'd be crazy enough to try to get to Angela or Faith out here at the Dry Gulch Ranch, where any one of us might see him?"

"No," Travis admitted. "Georgio normally plays it smart. No witnesses. No obvious risks. But if he thinks Cornell told Faith something that implicates Georgio in the smuggling or Walt's murder, he'll be desperate to shut her up. And Angela definitely knows too much, so he might be just as desperate to silence her."

"Time to take him down," Adam muttered. "And would I love to be the one who did it!"

Travis lifted his empty beer bottle in a toast. "Get in line, podner."

"Hate to break up a good battle-strategy session,"

Adam said a few minutes later, "but I've got two little girls who are hopefully ready for bed."

They all walked him to his truck. Travis, Faith and Angela waved goodbye to the others from the driveway.

The moon came out from behind a cloud and frosted the world in silver as they climbed the stairs to the porch. Faith waited for Travis to catch up with her, and he wondered if she had any idea of the sensual upheaval she caused him.

He should hate being here at the ranch. But how could he hate anyplace that included Faith? Unwanted urges surged, making his mind soft and his need rock hard.

Angela reached the door before them. "You have a really nice family, Detective Travis. You're lucky."

Thankfully, her interruption of his lustful thoughts cooled his desire enough that the bulge in his jeans didn't give him away.

"My family life growing up was far from normal," he answered truthfully. "But I am lucky that I didn't let my rotten childhood poison me on life."

"I wish I'd been that smart."

"You're young, Angela," Faith reminded her. "You still have time to turn your life around."

"Not if Cornell goes to prison for killing Walt. I won't deserve to be happy if that happens. It was my fault, even though if Cornell hadn't killed him Georgio would have."

"What makes you think that?" Travis asked.

"I heard Georgio tell him that one more screwup and there would be hell to pay."

"When did he say that?"

"Two days before Walt was killed."

That added a lot of weight to Travis's hunch that Georgio had been behind the murder all along.

"How did you ever get mixed up with a man like Walt?" Faith asked.

"He was big and tough and he looked out for me. I'd never had anyone want to protect me before. But then he started roughing me up and I knew he was just like my stepfather. Mean to the bone."

Kind of like Travis's early foster parents. Thanks to R.J. never coming for him and Leif after their mother died.

Angela opened the door and stepped inside. "I'm going to bed now, but thanks for everything, Detective and Mrs. Ashburn. I'll be praying for Cornell."

"Me, too," Faith said. She reached over and gave Angela a hug.

A nice gesture, Travis thought, a hug for the young woman who'd been the root of all Cornell's misfortunes. Faith was far more forgiving than he had ever been.

He walked Faith to the guest room. She lingered at the door, looking up at him in the dim glow of moonlight filtering through the window at the end of the hall.

A ravenous hunger that mere food would never satisfy rocked through him.

"I don't know what I would have done without you," she whispered.

"I'm glad we didn't have to find out." He trailed his fingers down her right cheek and the smooth column of her neck. He ached to kiss her, had to keep reminding himself that she was vulnerable, under his protection, nowhere near ready to deal with all that he was feeling.

And then she kissed him. One long, wet, sweet, tantalizing kiss that delivered a jolt clear to his toes—and elsewhere. He was on fire when she pulled away.

"Good night, Detective."

"That's it?"

"For now."

She backed away, closed the door and left him standing there. He walked away, still trying to get a handle on what had just happened. All he was sure of was that he needed a very cold shower tonight.

And tomorrow he'd need to find a way to prove that Cornell Ashburn was as innocent as his mother believed.

Without that, Travis might never get to see where that kiss could lead.

FAITH SLEPT LATER than she had in days. She woke to bright rectangles of sunlight pouring through the slats in the blinds and to the taste of the heart-stopping kiss still on her lips.

She kicked the sheet away and threw her feet over the side of the bed. The thrill of the kiss continued to titillate her senses as she padded to the bathroom.

Looking back on last night, she wasn't sure why she'd pulled away. She could have slept in his arms. Could have made love to him and woken up to his naked body stretched between her sheets.

But it wouldn't have been right. Not yet. Not with Cornell in a coma, not even aware that he was safe and home again.

When she made love to Detective Travis Dalton, she wanted everything to be perfect.

She splashed cold water on her face and smoothed her hair. She'd have breakfast and then see if Travis would drive her to the hospital.

Her cell phone rang and she hurried back to get it from her bedside table. She checked the caller ID. It was the trauma center. Calling this early had to mean something was wrong.

Her blood ran cold.

"Hello?"

"I'm calling for Faith Ashburn."

"This is she."

"I have good news, Mrs. Ashburn. Cornell has come out of the coma and he's asking for you."

Chapter Sixteen

Travis drove Faith to the hospital. They took the elevator to the trauma unit and went directly to the nurses' station, as she'd been instructed, and asked for Betty Norton, the head nurse.

The nurse was smiling when she greeted them. "You must be Cornell's mother."

"Yes. I'm Faith and this is Detective Dalton."

"You got here quicker than expected."

"I may have exceeded the speed limit a few times," Travis admitted.

"Are you a relative of the patient?"

"No, ma'am. I'm a friend of the family's, but I am with the Dallas Police Department."

"But you're not here as an officer?"

"Not this morning."

"I have to ask, because no one with law enforcement has clearance to talk with the patient yet—doctor's orders."

"He's only here as a friend," Faith assured her. "Is there anything else I should know before I see my son?"

"Only that the doctor does not want the patient to become stressed. Keep things on a light note. If he starts to get upset, I'll have to ask you to leave."

"I understand. May I see him now?"

"Yes. Just don't be upset when he exhibits confusion. That's to be expected. Even though he asked for you, he may not recognize you at once."

Faith hadn't thought of that possibility.

"Visiting times will be limited until his lead doctor indicates otherwise," the nurse continued. "You can have thirty minutes with him, but then he'll need to rest."

"How often can I return?"

"Every two hours, unless the visits unduly upset him."

As badly as Faith wanted to see Cornell, the warnings were making her increasingly anxious. She didn't want to do anything to cause him to suffer a setback.

Ten months without knowing where he was or if he was dead or alive. Ten months of longing to hear his voice. Now he might not even recognize her.

Travis took her hand, as always seeming to read her fears. "It's going to be fine. Just don't expect too much too soon. Give him time to open up to you."

"I'll try."

The nurse led them to his room and the cop standing guard gave them clearance to enter.

A lump formed in Faith's throat. She couldn't swallow. Her hands were clammy. Her stomach was churning.

Travis opened the door and silently nudged her inside with a hand to the small of her back. The nurse followed them.

Cornell's eyes were closed. The tube had been removed from his throat, but there was an IV needle in his arm. The monitors were on, clicking rhythmically.

"Say his name softly," the nurse urged.

"Cornell."

His eyes opened a slit. He closed them and then opened them again, wider this time. He looked from Faith to Travis but showed no sign of recognition.

"I'm your mother, Cornell. It's me."

He ran the tip of his swollen tongue across his chapped lips. The nurse dipped a cloth in a bowl of water and handed it to Faith. "His lips are dry. Why don't you wet them for him?"

She took the cloth and gingerly dabbed his mouth. "I love you, Cornell. I've missed you so much. I'm glad you're home."

"Mom?"

Her heart sang. "Yes, son."

"What happened to me?"

"You were in an accident, but you're in the hospital and the doctors and nurses are taking very good care of you."

The nurse smiled, patted Faith's arm approvingly and tiptoed out of the room.

"What kind of accident?" Cornell asked.

She looked to Travis. He nodded for her to tell Cornell the truth.

"You were shot."

"Why?"

"I don't know, but we're going to find out."

"Did you call the school?"

"The school?"

"To tell them I won't be there today?"

He was more confused than she'd guessed. It was as if he'd never left home.

"The school knows you're out," she said. "They said to take as long as you need to recover."

He looked at Travis. "Who are you?"

"A friend of your mother's."

"I've never seen you before."

"No, but I hope we're going to become good friends."

Faith had to smile at that. Her anxiety began to dissipate. Cornell might have been forced into a life of smuggling, but deep down he was the same as he'd always been. A good kid. With a good heart. He couldn't have possibly killed Walt Marshall or anyone else in cold blood.

When his memory returned, he'd tell them that. He'd explain everything.

"Do you think I could have a Coke?"

"I'll see."

"If not, just get me some water. My mouth feels like I've been eating sand."

"I'll bet it does."

"I'm sorry, Mom…."

"You don't have to be sorry, Cornell. Whatever happened…"

"Yeah, I know, not my fault. But if you have to take your sick days to take care of me, you won't ever get to go on that cruise to Bermuda you've been saving for."

"You take care of getting well, and I'll make sure she goes on that cruise," Travis offered. "Is that a deal?"

"Yeah. Deal." Cornell closed his eyes and drifted off to sleep.

Tears filled Faith's eyes as she wiped his mouth again with the damp cloth.

"He didn't kill anyone, Travis. We can't let him go to prison. You have to find a way to prove he's innocent."

"I'm working on it. All I need is proof of his innocence."

"You'll get it. As soon as Cornell can explain everything."

He was glad one of them believed in miracles.

"ARE YOU SURE you're not so hung up on this woman you barely know that you're feeding into her delusions?

"I told you, I'm following a hunch."

Reno shook his head. "If Cornell didn't commit the murder, what did Georgio use to blackmail him into smuggling the artifacts into the country?"

Travis pushed a stack of folders aside and propped his feet on his cluttered metal desk. "That's the little detail I haven't quite figured out."

"If that's a little detail, the Gulf of Mexico is a nice little fishing pond."

"My hunch isn't that far-fetched. Look at the facts I've put together." Travis pointed to a chart he'd hung on his office wall. "Up until the time he met Angela Pointer, Cornell had no criminal record. No juvenile charges. No school offenses. He's never even been suspended."

"Right. Good kid. I get that part of it. Kids can change."

"Walt Marshall is a hothead with a rap sheet long enough to paper your bathroom wall. Lots of people would probably have loved to put a bullet in him, including Georgio Trosclair."

"You don't have proof of that."

"I have no reason not to believe Angela."

"Except for her statement that Cornell killed Walt."

"She wasn't there when Walt was shot."

"Even if Georgio paid or persuaded Cornell to kill Walt, that's still murder."

"But what if he didn't kill him?" Travis argued. "What if Georgio or one of his paid thugs actually pulled the trigger and made Cornell believe he did it?"

"How?" Reno insisted. "By hypnotizing him?"

"I don't know how yet. I'm working on that, but it makes more sense than Cornell shooting some guy who was walking away. He wasn't one to look for trouble. He'd done a good job all his life of avoiding it."

"Like you said, until Angela Pointer came on the scene. Hot exotic dancer wanting him to protect her from big, bad Walt. Women can screw with your psyche. Like the way Cornell's mom is screwing with yours."

"I'm not getting screwed. Neither is my psyche. But I still say there's a knot in this rope the way it's hanging now. Cornell is a very unlikely murderer. Georgio is our chief suspect behind a string of murders."

"Show me the proof, Travis. You know I'd like nothing better than to put Georgio behind bars, but all we have to even link him to the smuggling at this point is Angela's statement. You know as well as I do that the prosecutor would tear her story to shreds in court. Not to mention that her version also includes the chapter where Cornell kills Walt."

"I haven't taken an official statement from her yet, nor read her her rights."

"Eventually, one of us has to."

"I know."

"To semi change the subject, how is Faith holding up?"

"Better than I expected, though I haven't seen much of her for the past two days. She's been at the trauma center, hoping for a memory breakthrough for Cornell. I've been working sixteen hours a day on this case."

"Maybe you should both take some time off."

Not a bad idea, and Faith was at the Dry Gulch Ranch this afternoon.

Travis dropped his feet back to the floor. "It's officially my day off and I've been on the job since six this morning. I think I'll take your advice and call it quits."

Reno grinned. "Don't blame you. Nothing like afternoon delight."

"I wouldn't know."

And unfortunately, he had no expectations of finding

out today. But if he hurried he might get home in time to go horseback riding with Faith. She had to be tired of staying inside the house and under guard anytime she was at the ranch.

More reason to find evidence to prove Georgio was responsible for Walt's murder. Putting him behind bars might be the only way to keep Faith safe.

THEY STOPPED AT the edge of the river, though it seemed far more like a creek to Faith Travis took her reins and helped her dismount. She walked over, took off her shoes and waded into the water. The icy temperature made her catch her breath.

Or maybe it was just being with Travis that had that effect on her. In barely a week, he'd changed her life. He'd found her son. He'd brought her to Dry Gulch to keep her safe. He'd been there every time she'd needed him.

The sound of his voice made her pulse quicken. His touch stole her breath. His kiss had completely undone her.

Faith knew it was too soon to be sure the relationship would last, but nothing had ever seemed so right.

Travis let the horses drink and then knotted their reins to the low-hanging branches of an oak tree. He bent down and picked up a fishing pole that had been left lying in the grass.

"This must be R.J.'s. The hook and cork are ready to go. All it needs is bait."

"He catches minnows in that net over by the tree trunk for that," she answered.

"Have you been fishing with him?"

"Today. One of the guards rode out with us."

"Catch anything?" Travis asked.

"Snagged a soft-drink can."

"That would have been tasty."

"I went wading. The water is nice." She stepped farther into the water that lapped the bank. "Take off your shoes and socks and join me."

"I'd rather watch."

Faith bent over and splashed water in his direction.

"I like R.J.," she said. "I know the two of you have issues, but he admits he's made lots of mistakes in his life. He's so excited to have Adam and Leif living at the Dry Gulch. He hasn't given up hope on the rest of you, either."

"Not going to happen, at least not with me."

"I don't see why not. You look, talk and ride like a cowboy. I could live here."

"In that case I bequeath my part of the ranch to you."

"I accept."

She waded back to the bank and dropped to a grassy spot in the shade of a gnarly oak. She stretched out on her back and made a pillow of her hands.

Travis kept his distance, though he couldn't take his eyes off her. He was mesmerized by Faith, from the perky rise of her breasts beneath the cotton shirt to the way her hair swirled around her narrow shoulders.

If he lay down beside her, he'd never be able to fight the unbridled desire ripping though him. If he didn't go to her, he was going to go crazy with wanting her.

He walked over and stretched out alongside, propping himself up with his elbow so he could look into the depths of her dark eyes.

This time he didn't wait for her to initiate the kiss.

Chapter Seventeen

Travis's lips touched Faith's, softly at first, their breaths mingling in a delicious blend of salty sweetness. Desire erupted in her blood, shooting her senses to dizzying heights.

The musky smell of him, the exciting taste of him, the intoxicating feel of his body pressing into hers… She closed her eyes and gave in to the thrill of him.

The kiss deepened until his lips had a ravenous hold on hers. His fingers slipped beneath her shirt and splayed across her bare back. His right leg worked its way between her thighs. Her body arched toward his, aching for more.

When his lips left hers, they seared a path down her neck. She turned and began to fumble with the buttons on his shirt, loosening them one by one until his gorgeous, golden chest was bare.

Travis returned the favor, kissing his way down her chest and abdomen until her shirt fell open. His thumbs slipped beneath her bra, finding and massaging her nipples until they were pebbled and erect.

She pressed against him and felt the hard length of his need pushing to escape his jeans. He reached down and unzipped them.

"I can stop if you say the word, Faith. It will half kill me, but I can stop if you want me to."

"No," she whispered, her voice hoarse with a driving need that wouldn't let go. "Nothing will change because we make love, but I need this. I need you. I need you so very much."

He kissed her again, but this time there was no holding back. He wiggled out of his jeans and then helped her out of hers. His hand found the inside of her thighs and his fingertips reached into her most intimate area, stroking the wet desire that had pooled there.

Then he lifted himself on top of her and thrust deep inside her.

She squealed in pleasure and then whispered his name with a moan.

His breath came in quick gulps. The thrusting grew faster and deeper and then he exploded inside her, taking her with him over the crest.

The sun beat down on their naked bodies as they lay in each other's arms, melting in the afterglow.

Nothing had changed on the outside. All the problems that had been there before were still present. Her fears for Cornell hadn't lessened.

But something had changed inside Faith. No matter what the future held for her and Travis, the moment had been golden and she would never be sorry for having lived it.

Love, however fragile and tentative it might prove to be, had found a place in her heart, and her world would never be the same.

"ARE YOU SURE you're calling me from a phone that can't be traced?"

"You know I wouldn't make a mistake about something that important."

"I never thought you'd shoot Cornell and leave him alive, either, but you did."

"It wasn't as if I didn't check. I was certain he was dead. The second bullet hit him in the back of the head. He went down. His eyes were rolled back in his head. I couldn't find a pulse."

"But someone did."

"And I'm doing all I can to make up for my mistake. I had someone hack into Cornell's online medical records. He's brain damaged. Even if he can talk, nothing he says will ever hold up in court."

"That doesn't make up for your mistake."

"I did some things right and you know it. We never would have found Cornell before the law did if I hadn't spread the word to all the ranchers in the county that I was looking for one of my wranglers who took off with an expensive saddle. Otherwise Billy Lewes would have called the police, not me, when he found that strange jacket in his horse barn."

Georgio couldn't deny that. But even if Cornell was as good as dead, Faith Ashburn wasn't, and she was as unrelenting as a Texas drought. She'd never give up on finding the man who had lured her son into a life of crime that almost cost him his life.

She'd fight the murder charge until she had the full truth.

"Did you get the information I asked for?"

"I did. Faith Ashburn is staying at the Dry Gulch Ranch with Travis and his dying father."

"And?"

"The old man rides his horse to his favorite fishing hole every morning after breakfast, occasionally alone, but usually accompanied by one of the wranglers."

Even as Georgio listened to the details Alex spouted, a plan formed in his mind.

He'd take care of Faith and then lie low for a few months, perhaps take a trip to Europe and let his new drug czar run his clubs.

Too bad Faith had to die. They could have had some fun together if she hadn't gone running to Travis.

On second thought, it wasn't too late to have some fun with her. The old guy might even get his jollies from watching them get it on.

FAITH WALKED TO the kitchen for morning coffee with a sweet ache between her thighs and a spring to her step that hadn't been there yesterday. She and Travis had shared the bed in the first-floor guest room last night.

They'd made love again—and again. They might have made it a third time except that Travis was called out on a homicide at the crack of dawn. It would be difficult to get used to hours like that. Not that she could afford to sleep this late every morning. It was after eight.

The coffeepot was nearly full, obviously not the first brew of the day. She filled a mug and went looking for R.J. Instead she found Angela in the front-porch swing.

"You slept late," the young woman said. "Five more minutes and I was going to knock on your door and see if you were okay."

"I was just tired, I guess. Where is everybody?"

"Joni's at work. R.J.'s gone fishing."

"This early?"

"He said it was going to rain later."

"There's not a cloud in the sky."

"I mentioned that. He told me his arthritis was a better predictor of the weather than clouds were."

"Then I better carry an umbrella to the hospital with me this afternoon."

"Where's Detective Travis?"

"On his way back to the ranch."

"Did he work all night again?"

"No, just from daylight on. Apparently, homicide detectives don't keep regular office hours. He's coming home to clean up, pick me up, deliver me to the hospital and then go back to work."

"I wish I had somewhere to go today. I love the ranch, but it gets boring. Do you think Detective Travis would mind if I tagged along with Joni tomorrow? She said it was okay with her."

"You'd best ask him that."

Faith's cell phone was ringing when she got back to the bedroom. She grabbed it from the dresser. "Hello?"

All she picked up was static. "Hello. Who is this?"

"Dizzy... Can't... Horse."

She could make out only half the words. "Is this R.J.?"

"Hurry."

The connection went dead. She kicked off her slippers and tossed her robe to the bed. In seconds, she'd pulled on a pair of jeans, a T-shirt and boots. She went tearing back to the porch.

"R.J. just called. I think he's disoriented. I'm going to find him."

"Not without me."

She turned to see Ray, the friendliest of the guards Travis had hired, standing at the foot of the steps.

"Okay, but we have to hurry."

"Do you want me to go with you?" Angela asked.

"No. You stay here in case Travis shows up and wonders where I am."

"Carl's checking the immediate premises," Ray said. "Holler if you need him."

Faith took off running toward the horse barn, with Ray right behind her. They saddled up two of the horses, mounted them and pushed the strong animals to a gallop.

Faith didn't slow down until she reached the spot where Travis had found the fishing pole yesterday.

A shot rang out. A cry of pain came from behind her. She pulled on the reins, bringing her horse to a stop. When she turned around, Ray was sliding off his saddle, blood soaking his chest.

Behind him, she saw R.J. tied and gagged and strapped to the trunk of a towering pine tree.

Georgio stood next to him smiling, gun in hand and pointed at her head.

"So nice to see you again, my dear. Here, let me help you off your mount."

She ignored his offered hand and dismounted on her own. "How did you get here?"

"By horseback, same as you. I just took a shortcut across a neighbor's pasture. I gave up on you calling me back, so I had no choice but to come to you. So here we are, together again, and with your omnipresent detective nowhere in sight."

Another rider appeared from behind a cluster of short, stubby cedars. He rode over to Ray, dismounted and tied the unmoving guard's hands and feet behind him.

"You want me dead, Georgio," Faith said. "Fine. Shoot me, but let Ray and R.J. go."

"Haven't you heard? I hate leaving witnesses around to clutter up a crime scene. But I won't kill them yet. They should stay around for the party."

"Is that why you killed Walt? Because you didn't want him to testify against you?"

"No, I killed Walt because he was a stupid jerk who didn't know when to keep his mouth shut."

"But you did kill him?"

"You surely don't think that prissy son of yours shot him."

"How did you convince Cornell that he was a murderer?"

"I hadn't planned to. It was serendipity. I walked out the back door of the club to see what the ruckus was about and found Cornell in the alley writhing, his eyes rolled back in his head. Having one of those seizures you kept talking about. And there was Walt, walking away, the perfect target."

"So you killed Walt, smeared his blood on Cornell and planted the murder weapon on him."

"Yes, and the beauty of it was that Cornell saw me as a hero. I got rid of the body for him and saved him from a death sentence. It took him months to figure out he was moving more than horses across the border. He was the perfect smuggler. He passed for innocent because he believed he was innocent.

"But enough about him. Let's get back to you. Take off your shirt first and then the bra. I love it when a woman's breasts fall free."

She slipped her hands beneath her T-shirt and slowly peeled it over her head. She couldn't die like this. She had to find a way to save herself and R.J. and Ray.

"Now the bra," Georgio said.

He was going to rape her while the others were forced to watch. Rape her here, near the same spot where she'd made love to Travis.

She couldn't stop him, but she wouldn't help him.

"The bra," he repeated. "Take if off and throw it to me."

"Go to hell, Georgio Trosclair. I'd rather have sex with

a snake than have you touch me." She straightened her spine and spit in his direction.

She was going to die at his hands. Finally, she knew her son was innocent of murder and smuggling charges, though it was too late to help him.

But Travis would discover the truth. Somehow, she knew that he would. She was glad they'd made love. Her only regret was that she hadn't told him how much she loved him.

Now she never would.

Chapter Eighteen

Angela met Travis as he started up the walk.

"Something's happened to R.J."

"Did you call for an ambulance?"

"No. He wasn't here. He said he was going fishing, and then he called Faith for help."

"Had he fallen?"

"I don't know. She just said he was disoriented, and she and Ray jumped on horses and went to find him."

"So Ray did go with her?"

"Yes, but I thought they'd be back by now."

"Okay, settle down, Angela. You know R.J. gets disoriented at times. Adam and Leif have told him not to go riding by himself. He does it anyway."

"I guess you're right."

"I'll call Faith and see what's going on."

"I tried that. She doesn't answer. Neither does Ray or R.J."

Apprehension set in. Travis punched in Faith's number as he walked to the kitchen and poured himself a mug of coffee. No answer.

And then he saw R.J.'s phone, plugged into the charger, half-hidden by the toaster. R.J. had not called Faith.

Travis shot out the back door and raced to the horse

barn. No time to waste on saddling, so he stopped at the corral, jumped on the back of a palomino and pushed it to the limit.

The neighing of a horse led him straight to Faith. He spotted Georgio and saw the glint of the sun bounce off his pistol. And then he saw Faith, on the ground, face-down.

The drug lord's right foot was crushing her shoulders into the hard Texas clay. The gun was pointed at her head. A young thug, also armed, was standing next to Georgio.

R.J. and Ray were tied and gagged.

Travis brought his horse to an abrupt stop that almost sent him flying over its head. One wrong move on his part and Georgio would pull that trigger. Faith would be dead.

How could Travis have let this happen?

"Welcome to the party, Detective. You almost missed the fun."

"You'll never get away with this, Georgio. This time you've gone too far."

"And what are you going to do about it when you'll be as dead as Faith? I've always been able to outsmart you and the other cops on the DPD. You know that."

"And you think no one will suspect you after Cornell links you with the smuggling and Walt's murder?"

"Cornell has a brain injury. You can't believe a word he says. And Angela. She's a stripper who was breaking up with Walt to get it on with Cornell. You'd expect her to lie.

"This all comes down to your poor old pappy and his deteriorating condition," the drug lord continued. "He lost it. It happens with those pesky inoperable tumors. He lured you out here, killed you one by one and then turned his gun on himself."

A guttural noise sputtered in R.J.'s throat. His face was bloodred. It was easy to see he was fighting mad.

"Keep your gun pointed at the detective, but take the gag from the old man's mouth," Georgio ordered his henchman.

The young man jumped to do as he was told.

The gag fell from his hands to the grass. R.J. let out a war cry that would have made Geronimo proud.

Miss Dazzler went wild. She stamped and reared up on her hind legs. Georgio dived away from her, trying to get out of her reach. The horse's front hooves came down on the drug lord's back and knocked him to the ground.

Georgio fired once. So did Travis, but his shot was the one that hit its target. It burrowed into Georgio's chest. He fell to the ground face-first.

The young thug tried to make a run for it, but somehow Ray rolled over in the grass and managed to trip him.

Faith grabbed Georgio's fallen pistol and pointed it at Georgio's accomplice. "Move and I shoot to kill."

"Good work, partner," Travis called.

"I'm learning from the best."

And hating every second of it. But if this was what it took to save her son, she'd fight the devil himself. Maybe she just had.

Travis tied up the accomplice while Faith freed R.J. Then she rushed to Ray and checked his pulse. He opened his eyes and tried to talk. Instead he only gurgled blood.

He was still breathing, but he was losing blood. She grabbed her shirt and used it as a bandage, pressing it lightly against the gunshot wound.

"I'm calling for an ambulance," she said. "Lie still and don't try to move."

R.J. shuffled over and checked Georgio's pulse. "You'll need a hearse for this one."

Once the accomplice was secured, Travis walked over and slipped an arm around Faith's shoulders. "Are you all right?"

"Not yet, but I will be."

"Good. Please don't ever scare me like that again. I was afraid I'd get here and find you dead, and then when I saw Georgio…" His voice broke. "Love can kill a man."

"Or save him," she whispered. "Especially when the woman loves you right back."

Epilogue

Two months later

The kitchen in the big house at Dry Gulch Ranch was overflowing with food of every description. Ham, smoked brisket, fried chicken, potato salad, purple hull peas, butter beans, corn pudding and enough desserts to fill a bakery.

"Where shall I put this banana pudding?" a neighbor whose name Faith had forgotten asked.

"There's room in the refrigerator in the mudroom," Joni said.

Someone else came in and added a plate of cupcakes to the mix.

A boy who looked to be about eight years old grabbed one of them and kept walking.

"Is it like this every Fourth of July?" Faith asked.

"Not according to Caroline Lambert. She says the local Cattlemen's Association's annual Labor Day celebration is normally held at the Oak Grove Civic Center."

"Why the change in venue?"

"There was a fire last month that destroyed the center's kitchen. Apparently R.J. not only offered to have the fire damage repaired, but volunteered the Dry Gulch for the celebration."

"That man never ceases to surprise me," Faith said.

"He's hoping you and Travis will surprise him soon with a wedding and a move to the Dry Gulch Ranch. He thinks ranch life would be good for Cornell."

"Did he say that?"

"He did. He's disappointed his other three children haven't come around yet."

"They still may," Faith said.

"They'd best hurry if they expect to get to know him while he's still healthy enough to interact with them. His bad days are becoming more and more frequent. Yet, weirdly, he seems more at peace every day."

"I think so, too. I like him a lot and so does Cornell."

A group of teenage girls wandered through the kitchen and asked where to find the soft drinks. Joni pointed them to a huge cooler on the back porch. "Let's get out of here and find a place where we can talk without constant interruption," she suggested to Faith. "I don't get to see nearly enough of you lately."

They moved to an upstairs sitting room.

"So tell me about Cornell. Has he regained all his memory yet?"

"For the most part. He's still hazy on a few things that happened while he was living in Mexico. The doctor has given him permission to start school next week and I've hired a tutor to help him with his studies."

"And Angela. Do they still see each other?"

"They stay in touch, mostly through social media. They both wisely decided they need to get their individual lives on track before they start making long-term commitments. She's living with an aunt in Kentwood, Louisiana, and is working to earn her GED. When she does, she hopes to enroll at LSU, thanks to a scholarship R.J. provided."

"And I heard on the news last week that Alex Salinger is cooperating with the police now that he's facing the possibility of life in prison."

"Travis said he's spilling his guts about the crimes he and Georgio committed, even the murders Georgio ordered to keep his drug-lord status secure. Walt made murder number six. His body was discovered last week."

"Travis must feel good about that."

"I think so," Faith said. "I haven't really seen that much of him lately. I never realized that homicide cops keep such long and irregular hours."

"He could probably take a desk job," Joni mused. "Leif says he has lots of seniority."

"He'd be miserable. He has the life he loves." There was just no indication it was going to include marriage to her.

And yet when they were together, he rocked her world.

"We better go back and join the party," Joni said. "It's about time for the president of the Cattlemen's Association to give his speech."

"That, I could miss," Faith admitted.

She ran into Travis on her way downstairs.

"I should have known you two were cooking up something," he said. "I've been looking all over for you."

"Am I missing something?"

"Yeah. Take a walk with me. I have something to show you."

"We'll miss the speeches."

"How's that for perfect timing?"

He grasped her hand and led her outside and down the path to the horse barn.

"Don't say no until you hear me out," he cautioned.

"You're talking in riddles."

"I get that way when I'm nervous."

They stopped at the door to the barn. "Close your eyes and hold my hand," he instructed.

"Wait a minute," she said. "If you're going to give me that abandoned black Lab puppy you found wandering around the ranch last week, the answer is no. My landlady forbids pets."

"No puppies," he promised. "Though you have to admit he's really cute and cuddly."

Faith closed her eyes and let him lead her inside. When he told her to open them, she was standing in front of a stall. A scrawny colt stood next to its mother.

"What do you think?" Travis asked.

"My landlady definitely wouldn't allow a colt in the house."

"It's not for you. It's for Cornell. I think raising a horse of his own would be good for him."

"If we lived on a ranch."

"Yeah, about that. I'm thinking of building a cabin here at the Dry Gulch. I know it'll mean long drives, sometimes in the middle of the night, but I can keep a small condo near the precinct for those times I can't make it back to the ranch."

"What does that have to do with giving Cornell a colt?" Her heart jumped ahead. Anticipation made her giddy. "Is this a proposal?"

"No. No way. Not yet."

Faith's spirits plummeted.

Travis dropped to one knee and pulled a ring from his pocket. "Now it's a proposal. But first the warning label."

"Okay."

"Homicide detectives make lousy husbands. They work weird hours. They get too caught up in their cases. They usually see more of their partners than they do their spouses. But if you'll have me, I'll work on being the best husband to you and the best stepfather to Cornell I can be.

"I love you, Faith, more than I ever dreamed I could love anyone. I can't imagine living without you. Will you marry me?"

"Yes. Yes! Oh, God, yes. I love you so much. I thought you'd never ask."

He slipped an amethyst ring on her finger. "I know this isn't the typical engagement ring, but it was my mother's. She gave it to me before she died. I'd love for you to wear it. Unless you hate it."

"How could I hate it? It's beautiful. And it's from you. I'll wear it forever."

Travis stood, pulled her into his arms and kissed her. Her heart sang.

"It's been a long, hard ride for me," he said, "but I feel like I'm finally home. Home to Dry Gulch and home to you."

"Home to love," she whispered. "And, okay, home to a newborn colt and a black Lab puppy, too."

One more Dalton son back in the saddle again and he wanted her at his side. She couldn't wait to start the ride.

* * * * *

REQUEST YOUR FREE BOOKS!
2 FREE NOVELS PLUS 2 FREE GIFTS!

HARLEQUIN

INTRIGUE

BREATHTAKING ROMANTIC SUSPENSE

YES! Please send me 2 FREE Harlequin Intrigue® novels and my 2 FREE gifts (gifts are worth about $10). After receiving them, if I don't wish to receive any more books, I can return the shipping statement marked "cancel." If I don't cancel, I will receive 6 brand-new novels every month and be billed just $4.74 per book in the U.S. or $5.24 per book in Canada. That's a savings of at least 14% off the cover price! It's quite a bargain! Shipping and handling is just 50¢ per book in the U.S. and 75¢ per book in Canada.* I understand that accepting the 2 free books and gifts places me under no obligation to buy anything. I can always return a shipment and cancel at any time. Even if I never buy another book, the two free books and gifts are mine to keep forever.

182/382 HDN F42N

Name _____ (PLEASE PRINT) _____

Address _____ Apt. #

City _____ State/Prov. _____ Zip/Postal Code

Signature (if under 18, a parent or guardian must sign)

Mail to the **Harlequin® Reader Service:**
IN U.S.A.: P.O. Box 1867, Buffalo, NY 14240-1867
IN CANADA: P.O. Box 609, Fort Erie, Ontario L2A 5X3
**Are you a subscriber to Harlequin Intrigue books
and want to receive the larger-print edition?
Call 1-800-873-8635 or visit www.ReaderService.com.**

* Terms and prices subject to change without notice. Prices do not include applicable taxes. Sales tax applicable in N.Y. Canadian residents will be charged applicable taxes. Offer not valid in Quebec. This offer is limited to one order per household. Not valid for current subscribers to Harlequin Intrigue books. All orders subject to credit approval. Credit or debit balances in a customer's account(s) may be offset by any other outstanding balance owed by or to the customer. Please allow 4 to 6 weeks for delivery. Offer available while quantities last.

Your Privacy—The Harlequin® Reader Service is committed to protecting your privacy. Our Privacy Policy is available online at www.ReaderService.com or upon request from the Harlequin Reader Service.

We make a portion of our mailing list available to reputable third parties that offer products we believe may interest you. If you prefer that we not exchange your name with third parties, or if you wish to clarify or modify your communication preferences, please visit us at www.ReaderService.com/consumerschoice or write to us at Harlequin Reader Service Preference Service, P.O. Box 9062, Buffalo, NY 14269. Include your complete name and address.

HII3R

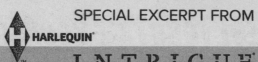
*Rachel Mancini trusted the wrong man—and nearly lost her life.
Now she's in the sights of a killer, and in order to survive she has to
put all of her faith in former SEAL Dylan Foxx. He's been the sexy
ex-lawyer's friend for years and will do anything to keep her safe.
And though it could prove fatal,
he wants her in his arms....*

Read on for a sneak peek of
EVIDENCE OF PASSION
by New York Times *bestselling author*

Cynthia Eden

"Dylan?" Her voice was so soft that she wasn't even sure he'd heard her.

He didn't respond, but he did lead her through the crowd, pulling her toward the door. Bodies brushed against her, making Rachel tense, then they were outside. The night air was crisp, and taxis rushed by them on the busy street.

Dylan still held her hand.

He turned and pulled her toward the side of the brick building. Then he caged her with his body. "Want to tell me what you were doing?" An edge of anger had entered his words.

Rachel blinked at him. "Uh, getting a drink?" That part had seemed pretty obvious.

"What you were doing with the blond, Rachel? The blond jerk who was leaning way too close to you in that pub."

The same way that Dylan had been leaning close?

"Now isn't the time for you to start looking for a new guy." *Definite* anger now. "We need to find out if Jack is back here, killing. We don't need you to hook up with some—"

She shoved against his chest.

The move caught them both off guard.

Beneath the streetlamp, Rachel saw Dylan's eyes widen.

"You don't get to control my personal life," Rachel told him flatly. *What personal life?* The fact that she didn't have one wasn't the point. "And neither does Jack. Got it?"

He gazed back at her.

"On missions, I follow your orders. But what I do on my own time… that's *my* business." She stalked away from him, heading back toward her apartment building.

Then she heard the distinct thud of his footsteps as Dylan rushed after her. *He'd better be coming to apologize.*

Right. She'd never actually heard Dylan apologize for anything.

His fingers curled around her arm. He spun her back to face him. "Your last lover was a killer. I'd think that you'd want to—"

"You're wrong!" The words erupted from her.

And something strange happened to Dylan's face. They were right under the streetlight, so it was incredibly easy for her to read his expression. Surprise flashed first, slackening his mouth, but then fury swept over his face. A hard mask of what truly looked like rage. *"You're involved with someone else? You're sleeping with someone?"*

Since when did she have to check in with Dylan about her love life? "He wasn't my lover."

His hold tightened on her. "What?"

"Adam. Jack. Whatever he's calling himself. He. Wasn't. My. Lover." There. She'd said it. It felt good to get that out. "We were going away together that weekend. We hadn't…" Rachel cleared her throat. "He wasn't my lover." She yanked away from him, angry now, too. "Not that it's any of your business who I'm sleeping with—"

"It is." He snarled the words as he yanked her up against his chest. "It shouldn't be…but it is."

And his mouth took hers.

Dylan won't let Rachel go, even if he has to
break the law in order to keep her safe….

Don't miss the next installment in **Shadow Agents: Guts and Glory,**
EVIDENCE OF PASSION
by New York Times *bestselling author Cynthia Eden.*
On sale August 2014, only from Harlequin Intrigue.

HIEXP69777

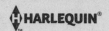